Dedication

This book is dedicated to the man who made such a difference in my life. You are the epitome of a true gentleman and I will cherish every moment we spent together. You will always be the love of my life and my heart will forever hold your face.

Sara's

JUN '10

Song

SEP 20

A Novel By

LESSY'B

JUN

My Time Publications
2984 Spring Falls Dr.
West Carrollton, OH 45449
www.mytimepublications.com

ISBN 13: 978-0-9843257-6-4
ISBN 10: 0-9843257-6-X
First Printing 2010
Library Congress Of Control Number: on file
Printed in United States of America

10 9 8 7 6 5 4 3 2 1

This is a work of fiction. Any references or similarities to actual events, real people, living or dead, or to the real locals are intended to give the novel a sense of reality. Any similarity in other names, characters, places and incidents are entirely coincidental.

JUN 2010

Acknowledgments

I'd like to thank the Holy Spirit for nudging me by whispering in my ear and for giving me this vision. It's only because of you that this dream is fulfilled.

To my greatest accomplishments, my children. To my lovely daughter, you have grown to be such a beautiful and strong woman. I am so proud of you. To my two sons, I am honored to call you my sons. I don't know what I'd do without you. Thank you for all the joy that you have brought into my life.

To my sisters and brothers, God definitely knew what he was doing when he put us in the same family and I thank him for each and every one of you.

To all my nieces and nephews, when I look at you, I see bright futures. Continue to reach for the stars. You are my heart.

To my aunts and uncles, thank you for being driving forces in my life. You have all been such an inspiration and I am blessed to be an extension of this family. I love you!

To the rest of my family, thanks for supporting me over the years and for always being in my corner. I love you all.

To Michelle Richardson, thank you for all your encouragement, advice and the "Idiots Guide to Writing a Novel." Your confidence in me goes without saying.

To my Best Friends Forever Sonya, Cynthia, and Cecilia, there are not enough words to express my gratitude to you. Thank you for pushing me when I didn't think I had anything left and for making me laugh when I really wanted to cry. My life would not be the same without you in it.

To my team of readers Cassandra, Rishana, Sonya, and Sharon, this book would not be what it is without your honest opinions. Thanks for keeping it real.

To my editor, Kathy Pattie, thank you so much for taking on my work and for doing such a good job. I couldn't have done this without you.

To all my friends old and new, thank you for touching my life.

To anyone I failed to mention, it was not intentional. Thanks a million!

Thanks to each and every one of my readers, I hope you enjoy the book!

To the loving memory of my parents:

Edith Williams and Rufus Fearrington

Your memory will endure forever

Prologue

The hot water running down my back felt so good after a hard day of work at the office. The temperature outside had dipped to a bitter nine degrees. When I stepped out of the shower onto my gray marble floor and looked around at my fabulous custom made bathroom with its afro centric artwork hanging on the walls, plants on stands between the shower and the 'throne', the maroon and gray marble sinks with matching maroon curtains, the step up Jacuzzi off to the side, and oh, I couldn't forget the sky light overhead bringing in just enough light to ignite the warmth already felt from the hot shower which was only a small piece of my immaculate twenty-eight hundred square foot Victorian style home, I became teary eyed because once upon a time, it had been only a dream. It took sacrifice, hard work, determination, and being down in 'knee bone valley' to overcome the many demons I had to confront and put behind me. Every time I got knocked down, which was quite often, I willed myself to get back up. There was little self-pity even though I asked myself numerous times, *why me?* But, instead of being defeated, I was the heroine because of it. I became a smarter, stronger woman. Not just physically, but more importantly, mentally.

Chapter 1

It was a dreary, rainy day in June of 1965 when Sarah Renee Johnson made her way kicking and screaming into the world on a dusty dirt road in North Carolina. She was a frail little girl weighing about four pounds, but she had a cry so deep and flung her arms and legs in a way that you knew she was going to be a survivor. Sara joined her three siblings; Adam, who was the oldest, then Angela, and JaLisa, who was three. A few years later, Terrance, Marcus, and Vanessa joined her. Her mother, Janet, had the children but her grandmother, Cecilia, who they called Mama Ce, was the one who really took care of them.

Janet was an attractive and smart woman, but had two weaknesses, men and alcohol. She spent most of her time at the local juke joint. She had all those kids but where was the daddy, or should I say daddies? Every one of the kids had a different daddy and as to whom each of them was, your guess was as good as mine. Because of that, they were shunned by a lot of the people on that dusty, dirt road. They were the bastard kids and had to carry that weight most of their lives, all except for Vanessa. Fortunately for her, she was born years later after Janet had finally gotten married. She didn't have to endure the hardships they all had to endure.

They all lived with Mama Ce, including their Aunt Wilma and her daughter, Katherine, who everybody called Kat. She was Sara's age and had no daddy, either.

♫♪♫♪♫♪♫♪

"It's my turn, it's my turn," I said as I anxiously waited for Kat to mess up in a game of hopscotch when I was about eight or nine years old.

"No it's not. My glass is in the block, not on the line."

"Oh yes it is, look. Your glass is right there on that line so now it's my turn," I said angrily.

She took her foot and messed up the lines in the hopscotch and tried to run, but I caught her and pushed her down. She threw dirt in my face as she got up and some of it got into my eyes, and boy did it burn. I grabbed her and pushed her down again. When she got up again and started crying and ran in the house, I knew I was in big trouble. She was the golden child who could do no wrong. She had the long hair and light skin. I was the complete opposite. I had cocoa colored skin and just enough hair to put in three little plaits, but even though we were both black, we were treated differently because of the color of our skin. It was bad when you were prejudiced against your own color.

"Sara, bring yo' ass here. How many times I got to tell yo' nappy headed ass to leave Kat alone? That's why you ain't gon' 'mount to nothing wit yo' po' ass." When I didn't move, she called again. "I said brang yo' ass here. Don't let me come down off this porch," she said, moving closer to the steps with a broom in her hand.

I didn't know why, but Aunt Wilma didn't seem to like me very much. I wasn't a bad kid, but remember, I was Janet's child, a bastard kid. I knew I was going to get it when I got there, so I took my time as I moved toward the porch. *Where is my mama?* I thought. As I approached the porch, I braced myself for her famous ear thump. I think I'd rather get knocked by that broom in her hand than to get an ear thump from her. I swear she could win an ear thumping contest. As I was about to approach the steps, I heard a car turn into the yard. When I turned around and saw my mama driving up, I ran toward her. I knew I ran the hundred yard dash in two seconds flat. She was not home that often, but that was one day she was right on time. Aunt Wilma turned angrily, glaring at me with those beady, bloodshot eyes of hers, and went back into the house while I stuck my tongue out at Kat who was sniveling, hanging onto her mama's leg. I knew when mama got into the house it was going to be on between them two.

Chapter 2

I really hated Monday mornings because it meant going to school. I liked school, I just didn't like riding the bus because we were the only black kids on it. There was an all black school, too, but Mama sent us to the white one because she thought we would get a better education. She said the white school was better with heat and air conditioning, better books, and better teachers, but to us, it was punishment. It seemed like every day my brother, Adam, got into a fight.

"Can I sit down?" I timidly asked a red headed, freckled faced girl who weighed about one hundred and twenty pounds, was only in the third grade, and was mean as a rattlesnake. Even though I was in the third grade, too, she outweighed me by about sixty pounds.

"Hell naw, yo' nigger ass ain't gonna sit here. Ya'll stink and I don't want you touching me. Ugh, get away from me anyway," she said, holding her nose.

As I moved to try and sit somewhere else, she stuck her foot out and tripped me. I landed face first on the floor and as I raised my head, I felt the blood trickle from my nose. When I finally got up, she hit me in the back of the head with a book, knocking me back down to the floor. The whole bus was gawking by that time. As I lay there, I wondered what she would do to me next. The next thing I knew, Adam had her by the hair and was slinging her from seat to seat. The whole bus was in an uproar by then and people were stepping all over me. They stepped on my hands and I felt a sharp pain in my ankle when someone stepped on it. I tried to get up, but I was pinned down.

Because of what she had done, Adam had to take on practically the whole bus. He was a rather thin boy, but he was strong. I guess it was from having to chop and tote wood, and from carrying buckets of water from the creek along with fighting them every day. He always beat the mess out of them.

"Slide over and let my sister sit down!" he yelled to the redheaded girl as he helped me up off the floor while looking around to see if anyone was going to object, which nobody did. When I got up, he wiped my face and I sat down. He stood beside me all the way to school. That was just one day. Tomorrow, next week, next month, we would have to go through the whole thing all over again.

♫♪♫♪♫♪♫♪♫

After school there was always something to do, but that day, Kat and I had time to play for a while. We didn't get along every day, but that day wasn't bad.

"Miss Mary Mack, Mack, Mack, all dressed in black, black, black, with silver buttons..."

"Ah, Sara, you messed up." Kat laughed as I hit her hand wrong during the chant.

"Ok, ok." I laughed, too. "Let's do another one."

"Let's do the one with the monkey," Kat said, still laughing.

"Ok. Three, six, nine, the goose drank wine. The monkey chewed tobacco on the streetcar line, the line broke, the monkey got choked, and they all went to heaven in a little row boat clap clap."

We were having so much fun. After a series of chants, we started a game of jacks. We played on the front porch of the old two-story house we lived in because it had fewer splinters. We were starting our second game when Miss Reva from down the road pulled up in her '63 Chevy to see if Mama Ce needed anything from the store.

"Hey, Katherine, how are you doing today?" she asked, walking up to the porch, completely ignoring me.

"Hey, Miss Reva," Kat replied as we continued our game of jacks.

Miss Reva was a short, robust woman. She was round in the waist and her legs were the same size all the way down, including her ankles. She didn't look that old, but her skin was aged from years of working in the field and she walked with a slight limp. She could have been a pretty woman if she combed and straightened up that wig she wore on her head. It used to be so crooked, sometimes I didn't know if she was coming or going, and every now and then, her false teeth would slip when she was talked.

"How was school today?" she continued.

"Oh the usual," I answered, trying to include myself into the conversation.

"Sara, I wasn't talking to you," she said sharply and looked back at Kat. We both looked at each other, surprised by her response.

"It was good, Miss Reva, same ole, same ole," Kat said. "Study, study, study."

"Well, that's what I want you to do, too. That's the only way you gon' be something in this world. Yo' education is very important. Hey, if you bring home good grades, I'll give you a little something for it, how about that?"

"I'm making good grades, Miss Reva. Will you give me something, too?" I asked excitedly.

"Sara, if you interrupt me one more time, I swear."

"Yes, ma'am," I said as I slowly got up off the porch. I didn't feel like playing jacks anymore.

"Katherine, I got to run to the store for your grandma, you wanna ride?"

Going to the store was a real treat for us because we never went nowhere but to school and church. Even if it meant staying in the car, it was still exciting just getting away from the house. The nearest store was about a twenty minute drive.

"Yes, ma'am!" Kat said, jumping up off the floor, dropping the jacks that were in her lap. "Let me go grab my shoes." It was nothing to go barefoot in the country.

"Can I go, too?" I asked with my fingers crossed and holding my breath at the same time.

"Not this time, Sara. We won't be gone long," she lied. People were always gone a long time when they went to the store.

"Yes, ma'am," I said, blinking back the tears that had started forming in my eyes.

As I turned and started in the house, Kat came rushing out. "You coming, Sara?" she asked with excitement.

"No, Miss Reva said I can't go," I said with tears streaming down my face. Her smile quickly faded because she thought we both were going to enjoy the outing. The door slammed behind me as I made my way to my room.

Why won't she let me go? I asked myself as I lay face down on the bed. *If she couldn't take both of us, she shouldn't have taken neither one of us. Now, I don't have nobody to play with.* I rose from my bed and looked out the window as they pulled out of the yard. Kat saw me in the window, waved sadly, and dropped her head. I felt so alone.

Chapter 3

A few years had gone by and just like every other day, there were chores to be done. Feed the hogs, go get firewood for the wood burning stove, and tote water from the spring, which was not a short walk. That particular day, I went to gather firewood by myself because the others had other chores to do. I went out a short distance when I saw Richard, a teenage boy who lived down the road from us.

"What you doing out here by yo' self, girl?" he asked, looking at me like I was something good to eat.

"Oh, I'm out gathering kindling for the fire, whatchu doing?" I asked as I continued to look for firewood.

"Well, Ma sent me out to get some wood, too, but I ain't in no hurry to get back. You?" he asked, looking at me devilishly. Richard was known as a bad boy. He had been sent to one of them reform schools when his mama couldn't do nothing wit' him. He hadn't too long got back. He was about sixteen years old, slightly muscular, and way taller than me and my seventy-five pounds, which I guess was average for a twelve year old. We didn't have no business being around each other.

"Yeah, I got to get back. They waiting on me to get the fire started, so I better be going," I said as I turned to walk away.

"Hold up, sweet thang," he said, moving in front of me. "I'll help you get the kindling if you let me touch you," he said, grinning like a Cheshire Cat.

I know he don't mean what I think he mean! That's supposed to be between grown folks, and the last time I checked, I sho' wasn't grown. Nervousness started to take over me. If I ran, he was sure to catch me. *What can I do?*

"Ah, Richard, you don't want to touch me. I ain't had a bath in a couple of days, so you know I stink," I lied, trying to keep him off of me.

"That's ok, Sara. I ain't had one, either, so we will just be two stinking people. Come here," he said, so close that I could smell his stinking breath. He was breathing heavy, and his breath was hot on my face.

"No, Richard, please. I just want to get the kindling and go home."

At that point, tears were beginning to form in my eyes. He grabbed me by the arm with one hand and slid the other into my pants. I was crying hard by then and pleading for him to let me go, but instead, he moved his hand deeper into my pants until I felt him touch my private parts. He was rubbing his finger back and forth until I felt myself in a way I'd never felt before. I stood there with my legs slightly spread, feeling helpless.

"Grown folks say this is nasty, Richard, please stop." I was crying loudly, but that seemed to make him rub faster.

"Be quiet!" he screamed, placing his other hand over my mouth. He was trying to put his finger in my privates but it wouldn't go.

"Ow, ow please, Richard, please stop, you're hurting me," I cried, but it was no use.

"Spread your legs a little wider," he whispered in my ear. "Spread 'em!" he demanded again. I slowly moved my foot out a little, then the other. I was beginning to feel sick to my stomach. I could feel his finger go inside me and it started to burn. "Have yo' boyfriend ever done this to you?" he whispered in my ear.

I looked at him like he was crazy. "Boyfriend?" I cried. "I am only twelve years old."

"Touch me," he said, pulling my hand to his private parts. I tried to jerk my hand away, but he was much stronger than I was and before I knew it, I had my hand on it, and it was long and hard.

I started to pray to myself. *Dear Lord, please don't let him put that thing in me. Please, Lord, please.*

"Feels good, don't it?" he asked, kissing me on the face and neck. He smelled like a mixture of beer and cigarettes. I wanted to throw up. Time seemed to stand still as he lowered me to the ground. No matter how hard I prayed, he kept on going. He made me take one leg out of my pants and pulled his pants all the way down to his knees, and then tried to put his thing in. He pushed and pushed, but it wouldn't go in. "Get up!" he said angrily. I was more than happy to do that. I got up and was about to pull my pants up when he said, "Suck it." My eyes got bigger than a fifty cent piece. I had never really seen one except on occasion when Adam was changing clothes, but I'd never gotten a good look.

"No, Richard, please, I have to go," I said nervously.

"You ain't going nowhere 'til you put this in yo' mouth," he said.

I was crying so hard by then and I could hardly talk. As he moved closer, I heard a stick crackle behind me. When I turned around, Aunt Wilma was coming our way. I had never in my life been so glad to see her.

"What in the world ya'll doing out here?" she asked, looking at me like I was enjoying what was going on. "Get yo' ass over here, Sara, fo' I take this stick and beat you. You gon' be just like yo' nasty ass momma. Take yo' ass to the house and you better have some firewood to get that fire started, too, you little nasty heifer."

"Aunt Wilma, I didn't do anything," I said as I scrambled to get my pants up. I was hurting in my private area. "I just came to get some..."

"Shut up!" she said, looking at me like she was going to hit me. "Ain't no telling how many times you done did this. You gon' brang shame to this family just like yo' mama. Git yo' ass out of here," she yelled as she walked toward me.

By that time, Richard had pulled up his pants and stood like he would take her on if she messed with him. I ran as fast as I could outta them woods, screaming for Adam. When he heard me, he stopped chopping wood and ran toward me.

"What is it, Sara, what happened?" he asked.

"I was...in the...woods...getting firewood when Richard..." That was all I was able to get out. Adam had taken off to the woods. I went over to the chopping block where he had been working, slumped down on the ground, and cried uncontrollably. I hurt all over. My private was throbbing from what Richard had forced me to do and my aunt had accused me of willfully participating in the act.

Couldn't she hear my cry? I wondered. *Does she actually think I was enjoying it? I never done nothing like that before. Why did he have to do that to me?*

I went in the house and put on some water to wash up. While it was warming up, I heard Aunt Wilma talking to somebody, telling them her version of the story. "I tell you, that girl ain't nothing but trouble. Watch and see don't she brang a youngin' up in here."

I couldn't believe it. I was the victim, twice. To Richard, and to Aunt Wilma and everyone else on Horse Shoe Road. All I was trying to do was get some firewood, that was all.

Adam came busting in the house and I could tell he had been fighting. He had a trickle of blood coming from his nose and from the side of his head. He grabbed me, hugged me, and told me, "You don't have to worry about Richard bothering you no mo'." I hugged him back, feeling relieved. I didn't know what happened in those woods, and to be honest, I didn't wanna know.

I went into the kitchen and put the hot water in the foot tub and took it to my room. It wasn't really my room because I shared it with my sisters, but at that moment, it was mine. I took my clothes off and stepped in the tub. The water was a little too hot, but I didn't care. I just wanted to wash that boy off of me. When I took off my drawers, I saw spots of blood in them. *Where is my mama?* I just wanted her to rock me in her arms and tell me everything would be ok, because at that time, in my world, it would never be ok again. When I finished my bath, I went to bed and that was one night I had no problem falling to sleep.

Chapter 4

A couple more years passed and things started to change on Horse Shoe Road. Adam had graduated high school and moved away. He said he hated living in the country and vowed to never come back. Being that he was the oldest, he took care of us the best he could. He had always been my hero and I missed him terribly. Angela was also about to graduate and go to college. Aunt Wilma met and married a man, Uncle Lewis, who was from up the road. She and Kat went to live with him. He was such a funny man. He used to play with us all the time. I guess since I had no male figure in my life, I became attached to him. In a way, I wanted him to be my daddy, too. I hated it when they left. I missed playing with Kat, too. She got on my nerves sometimes, but I missed her.

Being married must have been good for Aunt Wilma 'cause she wasn't so mean anymore. Believe it or not, I was starting to like her. They had moved to the big city and I hardly saw them after that. When things stopped going well between my aunt and uncle, she and Kat moved back home for a while. When summer came, Uncle Lewis wanted Kat to stay with him and since I had never been to the city, Mama and Aunt Wilma thought it would be a good idea for me and Angela to go, too. We were so excited. We rode the plane, and that was something else we had never done before.

Uncle Lewis lived in Chicago. I was fascinated by the huge buildings and long bridges. I could not believe I was actually out of the country and living a life I was totally unfamiliar with. The city was always busy and there were people everywhere. I never saw that many people in my life. Uncle Lewis was a short man, probably about five-seven, and one hundred and ninety pounds with a slightly muscular body. He had a dark complexion, a bald head, and big, pop eyes. He always wore a neatly trimmed mustache. Since he was a painter by trade, he would sometimes paint apartments in the building we stayed in after the tenants moved out. He used to take us to the park and to play with some of his friends' kids. I was having the time of my life. One day he had to go check out an apartment some people had just moved out of to see if it needed repainting.

"I wanna go!" me and Kat screamed, jumping up and down as he was about to walk out the door. Angela was a senior in high school, she could care less about going.

"Kat, you went last time. It's Sara's turn this time," he said.

"Yeah!" I said, hardly believing it. *Nobody ever let me go nowhere,* I remembered as I struggled to get my foot in my shoe. Kat wasn't happy, but she knew she was going next time.

We went up two floors and entered an apartment that had only a mattress in it. I followed him as he looked around the apartment. When we entered the room with the mattress again, he tried to pull me down on the mattress and kiss me. His hands were all over me.

Oh hell no! I said to myself. *This is not going to happen to me again.* I fought that man with every bit of energy I had in my eighty pound body. "Let me go!" I screamed over and over again while throwing punches, hitting him anywhere I could.

When he got tired of me fighting him, he let me go and started shouting insults at me. "Who do you think you are and where do you think you going, huh?" he yelled as I jumped up off the mattress breathing like I had gon' ten rounds in a boxing match. "You ain't nothing, Sara. Don't nobody care about you, not even yo' mama. All she cares about is that liquor. You'll never compare to Kat, she's gonna go places and do big things. You ain't going nowhere. All you know is them sticks back in North Carolina. If it wasn't for me, you would'a never seen nothing else. Now you trying to act all high and mighty." I did everything in my power not to spit on him. I was out of breath from wrestling with him and, believe it or not, I didn't cry that time. I looked at him disappointedly and turned to the door to leave when he said, "Wait, Sara, don't go yet. Wait 'til my peter go down, and please, don't tell Kat."

I looked back at him and walked out the door. All that played over in my mind was, *Wait 'til my peter go down.* It made me think about Richard and what he did to me.

"Is this how it is, Lord?" I asked as I looked up at the sky. "Is this how it is? Why they always messing wit' me? I ain't never done nothing to nobody," I screamed.

♫♪♫♪♫♪♫♪♫

I sat on the stoop for a good part of the rest of that day. I was ready to go back home. What could I do? I was helpless.

Kat came out and saw me on the stoop. "What you sitting out here for?" she asked, playing with a stick on the ground. When she looked up and saw the sadness in my eyes, she knew something was wrong. "What's wrong wit' you, Sara?" she asked again, looking me dead in the eyes. I looked at her and knew I had to tell her because I didn't want the same thing to happen to her because he wasn't her real daddy.

When I told her what happened, we cried in each other's arms. I told her to promise not to tell him. When we got into the house, we both tried to act like everything was normal. He was on the phone talking to my mama, telling her I was being very disobedient and wouldn't do nothing he told me to do.

"Hold on a minute," he said to mama. He waited 'til Kat was out of the room and asked me, "You told her, didn't you?" I looked at him and walked out the room. "Yeah, she is a bad example for Kat and I am sending her back home," he continued.

He did, too, and I was glad. I never told the grown ups what he tried to do to me. I knew they would never believe me. I did tell Angela, though, and that was it. When I left there, I hoped I'd never see him again.

Chapter 5

Later that year, Mama Ce suffered from a heart attack and wasn't able to get around much anymore. After school and during the summer, my brothers, Terrance and Marcus, and myself took care of her the best we could. We made sure she was fed and used the bathroom. Mama worked so it was left up to us to take care of her. My aunts came by and help out, too, when they could, but that was some hard work for us. It was a full time job for us and sometimes it got really tough. I missed my grandma, though; the strong woman who had taken care of us ever since I could remember could no longer take care of us or herself. She used to make us apple turnovers on the stove, laugh and joked with us, and she never treated us different. When she died that following fall, a part of me died, too. I never knew death until then and I found out how painful it was. It took me a long time to get it out of my head. I missed her so much.

♫♪♫♪♫♪♫♪♫♪

We used to walk up and down the road all the time with nothing else to do. We couldn't go nowhere. I spent a lot of time with Kesha from next door. They had just moved in, so we were just getting to know each other. She was a nice, shy girl with light skin. Not as light as Kat, but lighter than me and she had pretty, long hair. I was glad I had someone else to talk to. I liked her sister, Shelia, too. She was a year older and was nice, talked a lot of junk though. We used to get together every day after school and talk about what happened at school that day. We also had our share of fights as time went on and there was one I'd never forget.

"What you looking at?" I asked Kesha as I walked by her house.

"I'm looking at you, that's who!" she replied, rolling her neck.

"Well, why don't you come over here and do something 'bout it then?" I said.

"You come over here," she replied back.

When neither one of us made a move, Shelia, who had been watching us the whole time along with Marcus and Terrance, came between us and said, "Best man hit my hand." Shelia was a big girl for her age, and man, could she fight. She didn't start no trouble, but she never backed down from a fight, either. I hit her hand so hard, it stung. She hit Kesha and it was on for about two licks. Kesha hit me and I punched her in the stomach. She doubled over in pain and the fight was over.

As I turned to walk away feeling victorious, Kesha picked up a rock and drew back to throw it at me. "If you hit me again, yo' ass is grass!" she cried, and from the look on her face, I knew she would throw it. I stared at her for a few seconds, trying to act like I wasn't scared, which I was. I didn't want to challenge that rock because I knew it was gonna hurt. Shelia knocked the rock out of her hand and she went home crying. We were playing again the next day and became really good friends.

♫♪♫♪♫♪♫♪

Sixteen was an important number when you lived in the country. It meant a sense of freedom. I got my driver's license and my first job, Hardee's at Market Square Mall. I didn't have a car, but Kesha did, who was also hired, so we rode together. We were so excited. It was nothing like making your own money. Of course, it was minimum wage, but who cared? It was my money. I was able to pay for everything I needed for school, which helped Mama out, plus gave me some pocket change. I felt so independent.

There was a juke joint down the road that sold booze and played music on the weekends. That was where all the locals hung out. I was sixteen years old and was starting to look like a woman. I had filled out and had just started noticing boys, and boys were starting to notice me, too. That particular night, I wore bell bottom jeans that hung slightly off my hips with a white, short sleeved blouse that tied in the front just above my belly button. I wore big hoop silver earrings and a pair of brown platform shoes. My fro? It was put together. It wasn't huge, but every hair was in place. I didn't trust boys much after what Richard did to me, but they were becoming more and more interesting. I wondered what ever happened to him. I never saw him again after that day and I was glad. He probably went back to that reform school somewhere.

As I walked into the door, I noticed a tall, slim, dark skinned boy looking at me. He was kinda cute, so I smiled. As I danced my way around the room to the sound of *Flashlight*, somehow I ended up right beside him. "Hey," he said shyly, bobbing his head to the beat.

"Hey," I said back, feeling just as shy but still grooving to the music.

"My name is Johnny. Do you wanna dance?" he asked.

"My name is Sara and, yes, I would like to dance," I answered as we made our way to the dance floor. "I never saw you here before. Do you live around here?" I asked as we were dancing.

"I live in Maple Hill. I go to Maple Hill High. What grade are you in?"

"Eleventh," I replied.

"I'm a senior. Do you have a boyfriend?" When I said no, a big grin spread across his face. "What are you doing next weekend?" he asked, starting to sweat from the heat coming from inside the place.

"I work 12 to 8 on the weekends."

"Ah. I had thought about going to the state fair, and was going to invite you to go with me."

"The state fair? That's going to be fun. I don't have to work on Friday night," I told him.

"Well, do you want to go, then?"

"Sure!" I said excitedly.

"Ok, we can go Friday night. Where do you live?" he asked with a big ole smile, exposing all his pretty white teeth.

"I live up the road in that big, white house with the gray shingles on it. It has a big rock in the yard by the side of the road."

"I think I can find it. Ok, I'll pick you up around 5:00?"

"I'll be ready."

We danced a few more times and talked a little longer, but it was nearing the time for me to go home. "Well, I'm 'bout to go, can I get a phone number just in case something comes up?" I asked, getting ready to walk out the door. He gave it to me and I put it in my pocket.

"Ok. It was nice talking to you. See you next Friday!" he said as I waved good-bye.

♫♪♫♪♫♪♫♪♫♪

Monday morning came and I got on the school bus feeling good about the upcoming weekend. School had been integrated for several years by then, so the majority of the people on the bus were black. When I sat down, Drusilla, a big, dark chocolate, dyke looking girl standing about five feet eleven and a hundred eighty pounds of solid muscle, stood over me screaming, "You took my boyfriend!"

Lord knows I didn't know what she was talking about. I later found out somebody had seen me talking to Johnny that night and went back and told her. Word was he had just broken up with her and by the looks of things, she was not taking it too well.

"I don't have a boyfriend," I managed to say, nearly choking on the words. I really didn't. I had just met the boy a couple of days ago, but I *was* looking forward to going to the fair with him.

"You lying!" she screamed, getting closer in my face. "And, I'm gonna whoop yo' ass."

Thank God we were pulling into the school's driveway. It was so quiet on that bus that you could hear a pin drop. I didn't utter a sound. The only thing I heard was my heart beating out of my chest. I would rather be humiliated by being called a chicken than to get a major beat down by that big, Amazon bitch. What few friends I had were not my friends anymore. They all sided with her. They wanted to be on the winning team and evidently, it wasn't mine. She taunted me all the way to school and back, and I never uttered a single word. I had wondered why something that I had been looking so forward to all of a sudden didn't mean so much anymore.

When I got home from school, I called Johnny and told him I could not go to the fair with him. He tried to explain that he didn't want her, but I didn't want any part of him or her. I didn't know if he went to the fair or not, but I knew I didn't go with him. I should have though, because Drusilla didn't stop messing with me. She taunted me every single day for weeks. I didn't want to go to school because of it. It had to stop.

One afternoon she pushed the wrong button, Shelia's. Drusilla accused Shelia of being a traitor and challenged her to a fight. Unlike me, Shelia wasn't scared. The bus driver stopped the bus and they got off. According to those who watched, it was the fight of the century. I had already gotten off the bus so I didn't see it. I was glad, too, because after they got done, Drusilla probably would have beat on me. Nobody was declared the winner because they were both throwing some serious blows. That fight was the talk of Horse Shoe Road.

Later on that night me, Angela, who didn't take no junk off nobody either, Shelia, and Kesha headed for the V-Point. It was where everybody went to wash clothes because that was where the local Laundromat was, and to get knick knacks from the store. It was sort of hang out place. When you went to the V-Point, you were guaranteed to run into somebody you knew. Angela took a baseball bat and Shelia had a tennis racket just in case something went down.

Me and Kesha went empty handed because we didn't have no fight in us. Who of all people did we see? Drusilla and her older, bigger, and uglier sister, Maylene. I promise you they looked like descendants of King Kong. If I could have become invisible, I would have.

"Well, looka here." Drusilla said to Maylene when we walked in the store.

"Drusilla, you better leave my sister alone." Angela warned.

"Oh, un uh," Maylene said. "You better leave my sister alone. Didn't nobody tell Sara to go around taking people's boyfriend and if she gets her ass whooped, that's what she gets."

"If Dru can't hold on to her man, that's her fault, she better stop messing with Sara."

"Listen, bitch, you better get up outta my face," Maylene said, stepping to Angela.

"If you take one more step, I'm going to bust you in the head with this bat," Angela warned, raising the bat. When she did that, Shelia raised her tennis racket. Maylene shut her mouth and backed off. They paid for whatever it was they were getting and left out the door without saying another word. They stared and rolled their eyes, but said nothing. When we thought they were gone, Drusilla opened the door and yelled at me, "I'm still going to get you once we off school grounds."

I wanted to yell, "We off the school grounds now, bitch, now do something," but my nerves wouldn't let me. I knew I had to face her alone come Monday morning and I wasn't taking no chances. When I got on the bus that Monday, as much as I dreaded it, things were different. She didn't say a word to me all the way to school. It was the first time in weeks.

By the time we got to school, she looked at me like she wanted to say something, but didn't. By the end of the school day she walked by me in biology class and said, "Excuse me," as she passed, when she normally pushed her way by. She used to say nothing to me, just look at me like, 'Yeah, I'm gonna get yo' ass,' but by the end of the week, we were talking again. I didn't say we were friends, I said we were talking. I wished Angela had done what she did a long time ago because I had no more problems out of her after that night.

Chapter 6

It seemed like every weekend somebody was having a house party. A boy from school named Terry was going to be at one on that Saturday, and he asked me if I was going to be there. Since it was just down the road from me, I told him I'd be there. The yard was packed when I got there at around 8:30 p.m. I knew mostly everybody there from school. When the music was playing, the lights went out, but after the song was over, the lights came back on again. I guess the DJ did that to see what to play next. Terry and I didn't dance, we just talked. When the lights went out the next time, Terry grabbed my hand. We held hands until the lights came back on, then he conveniently dropped it and pretended to scratch his neck.

"Did you just drop my hand, Terry?" I asked in a surprised voice. He had been friends with Drucilla and her gang who were there at the party, so I guess he didn't want them to see us together.

"Ah, no, I didn't drop yo' hand."

"Yes, you did," I said in disbelief. "Listen, if you don't want to be seen with me, then you don't have to be!" I said and walked away.

"Wait, Sara, I didn't..."

"Save it!" I said, pretty pissed off. My cousin, Bebe, stood close by and I asked her, "Can you believe that shit? Terry dropped my hand when the lights came on like he was embarrassed to be seen with me. That's ok, you see Jacob over there wit' his fine ass? Watch this!" I said, looking over at Terry. "Hey, Jacob," I said, smiling at that fine man sitting on a rock, scanning the crowd. Jacob had graduated and was in the Marines. He was home on leave. I had seen him at school a few years ago but never said anything to him. He was a senior when I was a freshman. I thought he was the prettiest man I had ever seen. He had naturally curly hair with a caramel complexion and dark, deep set eyes with the thickest brows I ever saw on a man. He had small teeth with a little gap in the middle. He stood about five feet nine and weighed about a hundred and sixty pounds. He was looking good from head to toe. He wore a red checkered shirt with blue jeans.

"Hey, what's going on? I ain't seen you in a long time," he said, smiling.

"Nothing much, just trying to enjoy this party."

"You want to smoke a joint?" he asked, lighting one up.

"Yeah, I'll smoke one with you," I said as he took a hit and passed it to me. It wasn't my first time experimenting with marijuana, but I didn't smoke it often.

"Where you stationed at now?" I asked, passing the joint back to him while I choked on the smoke. Man, my throat was burning.

"Camp Lejeune."

"Oh yeah? I am going to join the military when I graduate. How is it?"

"It sucks if you ask me. You ain't yo' own person no mo'. You have to do what some asshole tells you whether you like it or not. When my time is up, I'm getting out."

"Oh yeah? I am going to try it and see how I like it. Ain't nothing going on 'round here and I can't afford to go to school. I want to do something with my life. I want to be somebody someday."

"You can be anybody you wanna be if you put your mind to it. The Marines just ain't for me, though."

I was really buzzing off the joint. "That was some good shit. Where did you get it?"

"One of my partners hooked me up. It is good, ain't it?" After that, it seemed like I giggled at everything he said. "Do you want me to take you home?" he asked.

"Sure!" I said as I looked over at Terry, who had been staring at us the whole time.

Right about that time, he came over and said, "Do you want me to take you home?"

"No, thank you, Jacob is taking me home," I said, trying not to bust out laughing from the effects of the joint. He just looked at me and walked off.

"You ready to go?" Jacob asked.

"Ready if you are," I said. He grabbed my hand in his and we left.

♬♪♬♪♬♪♬♪

"Oh, oh, Jacob, this feels so good. Don't stop, please, don't stop," I said over and over again as Jacob had my legs spread and he lay between them giving me pure pleasure. We ended up on a lonely, dark, 'lover's lane' type road and it was one time I was glad to be there.

"It feels good?"

"Ooh yeah, it feels so good."

"Turn over," he said in the most romantic voice. When I turned over and got on all fours, he entered me from behind. I had no idea it could feel so good.

"Ooh. Oh, Jacob," I moaned.

The louder I moaned, the harder he stroked. "I'm 'bout to cum, Sara."

"Not yet, Jacob," I said.

"Not yet?" he whispered. "Then, you tell me when it's ok. You tell me when."

"Ok." He stroked about two more minutes. "Now, Jacob, now!" I moaned.

"Here it come, baby, here it comes. AAAggg!" he said as he released himself inside me. His body started quivering and I could feel his heartbeat as he lay on my back. "Ooh, girl, that was good," he said, trying to catch his breath.

We lay there for a little while talking, and then we were at it again. We got out of the car and did it on top of the hood. He had both of my legs cradled in the crease of his elbows, and boy, he had me screaming. Partly from pleasure, the other part from pain. I had never done it before and I was beginning to get sore, but I let him ride. I had no idea smoking pot would have that kind of effect on me. After he came that second time, we got ourselves together and agreed to meet the next day.

♫♪♫♫♪♫♫♪♫♪

Jacob came by just like he said he would. We didn't do anything, just spent time talking. He would be leaving the next day going back to Camp Lejeune, but asked if he could come to see me when he came home again. "Un huh!" I said. "That would be great. When will you be coming back?"

"Probably next month. We got to go to the field for a couple of weeks, but when we get back, I'll be coming home."

"Ok. Look me up when you get back."

"Alright. Well, I got to get going. I still got to go pack. You be good, ok? Give me your address."

"I'll be right back," I said as I went in the house to get a pencil and paper. "Here you go, use it," I said, handing the paper to him.

"I will," he said, taking it and putting it in his wallet. He gave me a kiss and hug, got in his Pontiac Grand Prix, and drove away.

Chapter 7

Finally, it was my senior year. No more riding that damn school bus. Instead, I drove it, and boy was those some bad ass kids! I kept them in check though, and made sure nobody got picked on. I got paid for driving the bus, plus, I still worked at Hardee's after school. I was racking up money. I was so happy that I made it that far considering all the reminders that I wasn't going to be nothing. Nobody ever told me I could be something. So far, I had proved them all wrong and guess what? No babies. I wasn't a bad child, but it seemed like everybody wanted me to be. I think that was what gave me the strength to succeed. Nothing made me happier than proving folks wrong.

I had made up my mind about what I was going to do after graduation. I was going to join the Army. Nothing to me would have been more honorable. I didn't know any women who had joined and I was about to change that. I had always admired what they did for the men during the Vietnam War era and I wanted to become one of them. I really didn't have any interest in going to college, although I could write pretty well. We didn't have the money and even though I was smart enough for a scholarship, I didn't apply. I was going to be a soldier girl.

Jacob and I stayed in contact with each other on a regular basis. We wrote letters all the time and I had pictures of him pasted all inside my school locker. I saw him every time he came home on leave and our sex life got better and better. I was his girl and he was my man. He would be getting out of the Marines soon and moving back to the area. I was looking forward to it, but knew I would be leaving soon after graduation; moving on, making my own mark in this world.

♬♪♬♪♬♪♬♪

"Hey, are you going to the guidance office?" Kat asked one morning after the first period bell rang.

"No, why?" I asked. "What's going on at the guidance office?"

"Ain't this the day the Army recruiters supposed to be here?"

"Ah shit, I forgot," I said, looking down at my watch. "Yeah," I said, closing my locker and dropping books in my haste to make it to the office before they left. "Tell Ms. Jackson where I am," I yelled as I ran up the hall.

Boy, did I like what I saw when I walked into the office. There were two men in khaki uniforms with ribbons placed above their chests. They had on shiny black shoes and they stood tall and erect. They were both white and looked very professional. "Hi, my name is Sergeant Davis and this is Sergeant White," one of them said, extending his hand.

"I'm Sara Johnson," I said as I shook hands with both of them and then listened to them as they told me about the Army, the jobs they did, and the places I could go. I then set up a date for testing to see what jobs I would qualify for and agreed to take the test that Saturday morning. They were going to pick me up and take me to the testing site. I could not wait for the next two days to pass.

"Are you ready?" Mama asked as I waited for the recruiter to come pick me up.

"Yeah, Ma, I'm ready," I said nervously. My hands were sweating so badly I had to take some tissue with me.

"You'll do well, don't worry," she said with a smile on her face.

Looking at her, I could tell at that moment that she was proud of me. That was the first time I had ever felt that from her and I didn't want to disappoint her. She waited with me until the recruiters came.

After I got to the testing site, I went in a classroom filled with quite a few people who shared my desire. I was there about five minutes when the instructor began administering the test. I became really anxious when I noticed there were things on the test I was not familiar with. I had to pass though, if not, I wouldn't be able to join. When I finally finished, I had to go back out to waiting area and wait for the test to be graded.

After about forty five minutes of waiting in the lounge for my results, I finally heard my name. "Sara Johnson?"

"Over here," I said as I stood up waving my hand.

"Come with me," Sergeant Davis said as he led me into a room. "Have a seat. Congratulations, you did very well on the test. Now, I can set it up where you can go to Raleigh where all the in processing is done. They will schedule you a physical and help you select your job. After that, you'll be on your way. What do you say?"

"When would I be able to leave? I am still in high school."

"You can go in on the Delayed Entry Program. You can sign up now and wait up to one year before you go in."

"I don't want to wait a year. I want to leave right after graduation."

"No problem. Tell them that when you get there." Sergeant Davis said, smiling with his overcrowded mouth. "Do you want me to set something up for next week?"

"That'll be great!" I said, trying to soak everything in.

"Ok, I'll call you on Monday," he said as we rose up out of our chairs for me to leave.

Chapter 8

The school year went by pretty quickly. It was already April and graduation was the next month. I had just come back from Raleigh from taking my physical, which I passed, chosen my job, but most importantly, chosen my date to leave, which was August 19th. That was the earliest date I could leave for the job I'd chosen, which was a Supply Specialist. Jacob had already told me he was getting out in September, which meant we were about to go our separate ways. I liked him a lot, but it was my time to do something with my life.

"I leave in August," I told him one night as we talked on the phone. He hadn't been able to come home lately because he had been spending a lot of time in the field. He would at least make it back before I left.

"Wow," he said, sounding disappointed. "You'll be leaving right before I get out. Do you know where you'll be going?"

"I'll be going to Ft. Jackson for basic training and I don't know where I'll go after that," I told him, sounding kinda sad myself. I liked what we had, but I had a different dream from his. He was coming back to the place I was trying to leave.

"Do you think we can make this work while you're gone?" he asked.

"We should, but I don't know. Let me get there first. We'll see."

"Ok, babe, I gotta go to chow. I'll call you back soon."

"Ok, talk to you later." I was sad when I hung up the phone, but I knew my life was just beginning. I didn't want him or anybody else to change that.

♫♪♫♪♫♪♫♪

When Jacob finally returned home, for some reason, I didn't feel the same way about him. I was confused. I was about to leave. All I could think about was Uncle Sam. I knew it was just a matter of time before I left, so why continue a relationship that would be ending in a couple of months anyway?

"Come on, Sara, you know it's been a couple of months since I had some. Come on, girl."

"I don't want to, Jacob. I am not in the mood. Look, I really like you, but I just don't want to do this anymore."

"Well, if you won't give me none, I'll just go get some from someone else then," he said as he stormed out of the house. I felt sorry for him because I was his girl. I guessed it wasn't going to hurt if I gave him some one more time.

"Jacob, wait!" I yelled. I did give Jacob what he was asking for. I didn't have my heart in it like I usually did, but I did it nonetheless.

"I sure am going to miss you, but I am not going to try and hold you back. I hope you like it because I didn't. Watch out for the women, too, 'cause most of the ones I seen in there were dykes. They are gonna come after you," Jacob said as we laid there.

"I'm going to miss you, too. Adam told me about the women. I will be on the lookout. I will be back home before I go to my permanent duty station. I'll see you when I get back."

"Promise?" he asked.

"Promise." I smiled and kissed him on the cheek.

♫♪♫♪♫♪♫♪

We had just picked up our yearbooks and were about to go pick up our cap and gowns. It was a pleasure signing those yearbooks. Every signature in my book finished with *Have fun in Uncle Sam's Army.* I was so excited. August 19th could not get there soon enough. Soon we would all be going our separate ways, some to college, some to the military, and some weren't going anywhere. I was so glad I was not one of them.

"Congratulations, seniors. You've only just begun!" the principal proudly announced into the microphone. We all stood up, moved our tassels to the side, and gave out a loud cheer.

"We did it! We did it!" we all screamed to each other as we hugged and cried in the auditorium that Friday night. We all went into the gym afterwards to take pictures and to say a final farewell to friends and teachers we had known most of our lives. Now, we were going to go in different directions. It was a bittersweet night.

♫♪♫♪♫♪♫♪

I was a part of a college prep program called Moving Forward. It was a program formed to help students with their school work and to prepare them for college. It was designed for low income families and, of course, I qualified. We met on Saturday mornings and we lived in dorms on the UNC campus during the summer. We went to class every day just like college students. Our teachers were college professors and our counselors were college students. Last summer was my first, and this one would be my last. Since the counselors knew I was going into the service, they would run with me after curfew to get me in shape. We would run about a mile or so around campus and back.

One night after returning from a run, I went in to take a shower when I felt the urge to throw up. *I know I didn't run that hard,* I thought to myself. Anyway, I threw up and finished my shower.

When July came, I realized I hadn't had my period for the month of June. *Oh my God!* I said to myself because things were starting to add up. I never got sick after running and I never missed a period. *Please, tell me this ain't what I think it is.*

"Kat, will you go with me to the infirmary?" She was also a part of the program.

"What's wrong?" she asked.

"I think I'm pregnant," I responded shamefully.

"Sara, please don't say that. Maybe it's a bug."

"Yeah, a seven pound bug."

"Yes, I'll go with you, come on," she said, grabbing my hand. We had gotten really close over the years. Not only was she my cousin, she was my friend and my confidante.

I leave next month. Please, tell me this ain't happening, I prayed to myself. I went into the doctor's office while Kat waited in the waiting room.

"So, why are you here?" the short, bald, white man with a white lab coat asked me.

"I am here for a pregnancy test," I slowly replied.

"Do you want to be pregnant?"

"No, sir. I leave next month going into the military. I do not want to be pregnant," I said as my eyes started to fill with water.

"Ok, well what I want you to do is go in that bathroom and urinate in this cup. Leave it there and then come back out here."

"Ok," I said as I went into a bathroom so small I could hardly turn around.

After about thirty minutes, the doctor came back into the room and I could tell by the look on his face that it was not good news. He looked me and said the most heartbreaking news I had ever heard, "You're pregnant."

I immediately started crying. *How could this happen to me? How?* I asked myself. The deliverer of the bad news left the room to give me a few minutes alone. As I turned to look out the window, it was raining so hard it made me cry even harder. The only thing that went through my mind was, *You ain't gon' 'mount to nothing. See won't she brang some youngins up in here.* They were right after all. I wasn't going to be nothing. That was the darkest day of my life. I could kiss all my dreams good bye.

Chapter 9

"Get away from me!" I yelled to Jacob as I ran into the dorm room. He had come to visit me, but I had not yet told him the disappointing news.

"What is wrong with you, Sara? What did I do?" he asked with sheer concern on his face.

"You ruined my life, that's what. Stay as far away from me as you can!" I yelled through the now closed door.

It had been three days since I found out I was pregnant. I was so depressed; I only came out of my room to use the bathroom. Kat would bring me something to eat from the cafeteria and I avoided Jacob like the plague. *I knew I shouldn't have given in that night. If I had only kept my drawers up, this would not be happening. Where can I get rid of it?* I asked myself frantically. *I cannot let this ruin my life.* My head hurt me so bad. Everything I ate came right back up. I was miserable. What was I going to do? Oh, you could best believe Kat was going to college. Everything was playing out just as predicted.

"Sara, please open the door and talk to me," Jacob pleaded.

"What?" I yelled to him as I opened the door. "Say what you got to say and leave, ok?"

"Baby, what is it? What did I do?"

"What did you do? I'll tell you what you did. You ruined my life, that's what you did. You know why? Because I'm pregnant, that's why. Now, leave me alone!"

Before I could close the door to my room, he grabbed my arm and pulled me to him. "You're pregnant? That's good news!"

That man must have just got done smoking a joint.

"How is that good news, Jacob? My life is ruined."

"No, it's not. I'll re-enlist. We can get married and you can travel with me. Please, baby, I want to be with you."

"Bye, Jacob," I said as I walked back into the room and closed the door.

"Sara, please, think about what I said," he yelled through the closed door. I didn't say anything as I heard him walk away. My head was spinning so badly, I had to sit down.

Word had already circulated around campus. People were looking at me whispering, and my friends acted like they had to think of things to say to me instead of our usual conversations.

"I am just pregnant!" I yelled in the hallway one day. "It's not contagious." I really didn't care anymore.

Michelle, one of the counselors, always came by my room to see how I was doing. "It's going to be ok, you know. I know you are under a lot of pressure right now and I'm sorry you have to go through this, but God will make a way if you trust Him. Things happen for a reason. Jacob sounds like he loves you. Do you love him?"

"I don't know, Michelle. I want to, but I blame him for this."

"Did he rape you?" she asked.

"No."

"So, what is your part in this?"

"I know what you're trying to say, Michelle, but I really don't want to hear this right now. All I know is all my life I've had to prove that I was just as good as everybody else. I have always had to work harder just to get acceptance in my own family. I've always felt like the ugly duckling. Now look. I really ain't nothing."

"As long as you believe that, that's all you'll ever be," she said. "I got to go now, but I'll be back to check on you." She reached down and gave me a big hug.

"Thanks, Michelle, I needed that."

"Anytime." She smiled as she touched my chin with her finger. "See you later."

Jacob came by the next day. "How you doing?" he asked as he awkwardly walked into the room.

"I don't know, but I guess I'll make it. I am going to keep the baby, Jacob, but you know I can't join the Army pregnant, right? I want you to keep your word. Re-enlist and marry me. Will you do that?"

"Yes, I'll do that," he said as he came closer to give me a hug.

I backed away. "Uh uh, that's how I got in trouble in the first place."

"So, what harm can we do now?" he asked.

"None, I guess," I said as I relaxed in his arms. "None."

He squeezed me and kissed me on the forehead. "I'll take care of you."

"I hope so, Jacob. I sure hope so."

I didn't see Kat often after that summer. She went off to college like most of my friends did and I joined the ranks of the ones who weren't going to do anything after graduation. You have no idea how painful that was. I wasn't mad at her, though, in fact, I was happy for her. She was doing what she wanted to do and I hoped she was successful at whatever she became.

Chapter 10

Angela was attending Virginia Tech and was expecting her first child, too. I went to stay with her because I had no job, no car, and no means of survival. Jacob didn't re-enlist because he said he waited too late and since he was starting over, he had no job, either. As soon as he got one and on his feet, he said he would come get me and we would get married. I got a job working at good old Hardee's. That time, I wasn't thrilled about it. I had called my recruiter a month or so earlier and told him about my situation. I had to go back to Raleigh and fill out some paperwork to get me out of my contract. That was one trip I really dreaded taking. Now look at me. Going in a direction I didn't know where I'd end up when I should have been in basic training. *Things happen for a reason.* Yeah right. I couldn't wait to find out what the reason for me getting pregnant was.

It was getting close to Christmas and Angela and I were looking forward to spending it together. I didn't see Jacob that often anymore since I stayed so far away and he still hadn't got a job.

♫♪♫♪♫♪♫♪♫

"Hey, girl, what's going on?" my sister, JaLisa, called me one day and asked. JaLisa was still living back home. She had gotten married, but it didn't work out. She had a daughter, Jamacia, and they were doing pretty good. She liked living back home. She liked being close to the family and let me tell you, she was full of drama.

"Not a lot, taking things day by day. What's up?"

"I was just wondering if you had heard from Jacob lately."

"I heard from him a couple of days ago. Why?" I asked, wondering why she would be asking me about Jacob.

"Well, Saturday night I went to the Big No Show," that was a juke joint back home, "and he was there talking to Diane Jones. He was all up in her face and she was just grinning. I walked by them thinking that if she saw me, she would stop, but she kept right on grinning. I wanted to bust her right in her Porky the Pig looking face. I went to the bar to get a drink and when I came back, they were gone. So, I went outside to see if they were out there. That's when I saw her getting into his car and they left."

"Are you sure?" I asked, starting to feel nauseous.

"Yeah, 'cause as he was backing out the driveway, he got stuck in a ditch. It took about four people to pull him out and when they got him out, how 'bout them fools got stuck right back in the same spot? Everybody saw them."

I really didn't want to hear anymore. *That son of a bitch. Look at this shit. I gave up everything because I believed this man.* "I'm on my way back to North Carolina."

"No, you not," Angela said, coming from the back room. She didn't know everything that was said, but enough to know that something smelled like a rat. "First of all, you don't believe everything people tell you. Wait 'til you talk to Jacob before you take yo' pregnant ass down there. See what he has to say."

"You know he ain't gonna say he did it. Would you? He gonna deny it and try to make somebody else look like the bad guy."

"How you gonna get down there? You know you ain't got no money."

"I'll catch a bus."

"Where you gonna stay?"

"I don't know."

"Exactly. Now get yo' ass somewhere and sit down. He'll call and when he does, you'll get to the bottom of it. Let me have that phone. JaLisa? Don't you call here no mo' wit' that shit," she said and hung up the phone.

I cannot believe this is happening, I said to myself as I lay on the bed crying. *What am I going to do? I am too far along to have an abortion. I don't want to give it up for adoption. Oh Lord, what am I gonna do? This man has told me nothing but lies. I trusted him, Lord. What am I gonna do with the rest of my life? It is just beginning, and it is not starting off too good. I am never going to get ahead. I'm going to always be held back and have to scrape to survive. Lord, please help me!*

♫♪♫♪♫♪♫♪♫

"Will you get that, Sara?" Angela yelled when the phone rang. She lived in a two bedroom, one bath trailer in Wilson Trailer Park. Even though it was a trailer park, it was always kept clean. She rented it when she was in school because it was affordable. She had a roommate from time to time to help pay the expenses. I slept on the couch most of the time, but every now and then I did get to sleep in a bed.

"Yeah, I got it. Hello?"

"Hey, what's up?" Jacob asked.

"I don't know, Jacob, you tell me."

"Who is it?" Angela yelled again.

"It's for me," I yelled back.

"Not a lot, missing you."

"Oh really? Is that why you were with Diane Jones Saturday night?"

"Now, where in the world did you get that from? I wasn't wit' no Diane."

"Did you go to the Big No Show?"

"Yeah, I went, but I wasn't wit' nobody."

"So, you left by yourself?"

"Naw, ahh, I was getting ready to leave and Diane asked me if I would drop her off by her house. I said yeah since I was going that way. That's all I did, just dropped her off."

"So, you are the only one who could have done that, Jacob? Don't forget I am stuck here with this baby in my stomach that you begged me to have and promised to take care of. Is this how you gon' take care of us? 'Cause if it is, I don't want you to. You can have Diane and any other pig faced bitch you want. I am not going to let you make a fool of me. I am dealing with enough to have to be dealing wit' yo' shit, too. Do you hear me? You didn't have no business wit' no other woman in that car."

"Hold up. I said I didn't do nothing."

"Oh yeah? Who do you want me to ask, Diane? What she gonna say? 'Naw we didn't do nothing.' Yeah right, Jacob. Let me tell you this. If I hear that you been riding anybody else in that car, you will never see me nor this baby, you understand?"

"Yeah, but you making a big deal out of nothing."

"Oh, am I? Let it happen again and I'll show you how big a deal I can make out of it. You got a job yet?"

"Naw. I'm waiting for these people to call me. When you coming back this way?"

"Why, so you can plan yo' shit around me?"

"You know what, Sara, I didn't call you for this shit. If this is all you gon' talk about, I'll talk to you later."

"Bye!" I said and hung up the phone. Sorry ass bastard. I done sacrificed my dreams for that man and he thought he was gon' treat me like shit? We'd see.

♫♪♫♪♫♪♫♪♫♪

"Let's go to the hospital," Angela said as she came down the hall holding her stomach. The doctor did say she was due anytime, I guess it was time. She was in a sorry relationship, too. She met a guy in college who was supposed to care about her. When he found out she was pregnant, he disappeared. She didn't know where he was or where to find him. Now, she had to go through it all by herself. Some men were sorry as hell. All they wanted was to fuck, and that was it. They didn't want the responsibility that came with it. As long as 'Mr. Happy' was satisfied, they didn't care about nothing or nobody else. I found that out the hard way.

"Push!" the doctor told her in the delivery room after we had been there for twelve hours.

"I am!" she screamed. I was so scared. I was going to have to go through the same thing in a few months. She was in so much pain. I tried to wipe the sweat from her forehead, but every time I'd get close to her she would have another contraction and start acting belligerent. I went and stood by the doctor. It was safer there.

"Here it comes!" I told her, feeling my adrenaline starting to rise. "I see the head!"

"Ok, one more push should do it. Now, give me a good strong push," the doctor said. Angela pushed so hard, I thought a vessel was going to pop in her head, but out came a beautiful baby boy.

"He is beautiful," I told her as the doctors were cleaning him up. I wondered, *What is my baby gonna look like? I hope it's healthy. I'll see in a few months.*

♫♪♫♪♫♪♫♪

Jacob came to see me during Christmas. We had an ok time, but I still kept thinking about him and Diane. It was hard for me to have sex with him because all I could think about was him having sex with her. I knew I didn't look like much, but I felt like a beauty queen next to her. She was chubby with no shape at all, absolutely no butt and I knew the inside of her thighs rubbed together when she walked. Plus, her feet turned in. Her eyes were spaced far apart and her nose was wide and turned up like a pig. In school, they called her Snouty. Another point; some men didn't care what you looked like. It was all about 'Mr. Happy.'

"When are you coming back home?" Jacob asked.

"Probably next month. I want to come home and have the baby. Jacob, what are we going to do? Where am I supposed to stay?

If I go to Mama's, I will have to sleep in the living room 'cause there is not enough room for us. I am tired of sleeping on the couch. My back hurts all the time. You ain't found a place yet?"

"No, I'm still looking, though. I just started this job, so hopefully, things will start looking up soon."

"I hope so. I want to take this baby to our house, not some place where we might have to sleep on the couch. People will be coming in at all times of the night. We won't have no privacy."

"I'm working on it, ok?"

"Ok," I said sadly. Here I was about to have a baby with no place to go. I was homeless and pregnant. That was definitely not how I'd planned my life.

Chapter 11

February 18th came and went. That was the day my baby was due. I had since moved back to stay with my mama and, luckily, I didn't have to sleep on the couch. I didn't like staying there because of all the drinking, but what choice did I have? If you had ever been around people who drank, you knew what I was talking about. Sometimes there was food to eat and sometimes there wasn't. I stayed in my room most of the time. Jacob still hadn't gotten himself together. He was still living at home with his mama. I couldn't understand how a grown man could live at home. I really thought it was because they were too cheap to move out, afraid of life's responsibilities.

It had been several months since he had gotten out of the military and we were no closer to marriage than we were that day he told me he'd marry me. I often imagined what my life would be like if I was in the Army. Where would I be and what would I be doing? I would never know. I was only punishing myself by thinking about it. One thing I did know was that I wouldn't wish that situation on anybody, but I knew things had to get better one day. I wasn't giving up.

"I think it's time," I told Jacob one day when he came by after work.

"Are you sure?"

"Yes, I'm sure. It hurts so bad." We were getting close to March. I knew I wasn't gonna carry the baby forever. If it wasn't the time, I was going to perform my own surgery.

"Ok, let's go. I'm going to call Mama and let her know we are on our way to the hospital. She can meet us there," he said.

"Alright," I said, trying to make my way to the front door. I doubled over twice before I got there. Mama helped me to the car.

Let me tell you about his mama, Lucy. She was something special. She treated her children like they were babies and they were all grown except for one. She was light skinned and a rather robust woman, very pretty. Her hair hung way down her back and she could cook better than any woman I knew except Mama. She thought her family was better than everybody else. A lot of folks were surprised when I started dating Jacob because my hair wasn't long and my skin wasn't light. I didn't know what I did to get him, either, but you didn't know how many times I wished I didn't. He did everything his mama said, whether I liked it or not. She had control over him, and as long as she helped pay their bills, they didn't mind.

When we got to the hospital, the nurse told me I was having false labor and was sending me back home. "False labor! Ain't nothing false about this pain I'm in!" I screamed to the middle aged woman who had checked me.

"I'm sorry, ma'am, but you're going to have to come back. Keep walking, it will speed up your contractions."

I was so mad. "You mean to tell me it's going to hurt worse than this?" I asked.

"Ma'am, you are only two centimeters. You have to be at least three before we can admit you. Go walking for a while and I'm sure you will have the baby soon."

I walked around the hospital for four hours and when the pain had gotten much worse, I went back to the labor and delivery floor.

"Ok, you are three centimeters. We can admit you now," she said.

"Four hours of walking and I only went one centimeter?" I asked in disbelief. I knew right away I was in for a long night.

Once I was admitted, I was put in a room that had a lot of scary looking machines. I was hooked up to two different ones, plus, they put an IV in my arm. One of the machines they hooked me up to monitored the baby's heart beat and it was such a wonderful sound.

"Oh, it hurts," I screamed to Jacob as I felt another contraction. They were coming pretty regularly.

"It won't be long now, just hang in there," he said.

"That's easy for you to say, you're not the one lying here suffering. Oh, it hurts. Doctor, is there anything you can give me for this pain?"

"If your water had broken, I could give you an epidural, which would numb you from the waist down. If you were four centimeters, we could break your water and give it to you, but you are still only three centimeters."

"Dammit, there is always a catch. I can't take this. It hurts too bad."

"I'm sorry, ma'am, there's nothing we can do," she said, looking at me pitifully.

She left the room and I was left there to endure the grueling pain. I moaned and groaned, and there was nothing nobody could do about it. Jacob tried to console me, but he was no help. About an hour later, I let out a loud scream and she came back into the room.

"Ma'am, you're going to have to keep it down. You are scaring the other patients," she said.

"I don't care. I cannot take this pain," I screamed at her. "Please, do something."

She went down to the bottom of the bed and checked me again. "She is still only three centimeters, but I am going to stretch her to four and break her water. I can't have her in here scaring the other patients," she whispered to her assistant with an annoyed look on her face. I didn't care how annoyed she was, the pain was unbearable. My only consolation was hearing my baby's heart beat on that monitor. "Ok, this shot is going to go into your spine, so you'll have to be really still because if you move, it could paralyze you. All you have to do is sign this consent form and you'll be all set," she said, handing me a clipboard.

After I signed it, she brought over a tray with a long needle on it and I immediately became anxious. *What if I move? Lord, please, help me be still.*

"Ok, now I need you to sit up," she said. With Jacob's and the assistant's help, I sat up and prepared myself for what was about to happen. "Now, when you have your next contraction, let me know. That's when I'll give you the injection."

"That's crazy, how do you expect me to be still with so much pain? I don't know if I should do this," I said.

"The pain is only going to get worse, Ms. Johnson. I have given these shots many times and I have never paralyzed anyone. Just be really still and your pain will soon be over," she said, trying to reassure me.

I took a deep breath and waited for the contraction. "Here it comes," I moaned.

"Ok, be really, really still," she said, easing the needle in my back. I sat as still as I possibly could. I felt the needle go in and before I knew it, it was over. "You should start feeling better now, Ms. Johnson," she said, pushing the tray away. "Now, lie down and get comfortable," she said, pulling the covers up on me.

I did feel better. I didn't feel another contraction. I was able to lie there and listen to my baby's heart beat pain free.

"I'm gonna go out and give Mama and 'em an update," Jacob said, referring to Mama and JaLisa who had since joined Lucy. "I'll be back in a few, ok?" Jacob said, opening the door.

"Alright," I said, trying to get comfortable. "Tell Mama to go on home and I'll call her when the baby comes."

"Ok," he said, walking out.

♫♪♫♪♫♪♫♫

I had laid there for several hours waiting and listening to my baby's heartbeat. Ms. Lucy had gone home, too, to cook and would be coming back soon. Jacob had gone to sleep in a nearby chair. I was doing fine until I stopped hearing my baby's heartbeat on the monitor. I rang for the nurse and when she came in, I yelled, "I can't hear my baby's heartbeat anymore."

She looked at the monitor and yelled, "Code blue!" All of a sudden, things started moving in slow motion. Five doctors came running into the room.

"Turn over and get on all fours," she yelled hysterically. Two of the doctors helped me turn over. Once on all fours, the nurse inserted her hand inside my vagina.

"What's going on?" I asked in a panic.

"I am massaging your uterus. Your baby is losing oxygen and I don't know why." While she was massaging, it seemed like every doctor in the hospital was looking at my butt. I felt so uncomfortable, especially being on all fours. Within a minute or so, the heart monitor started to beat again. I breathed a deep sigh of relief, and so did everyone else.

"You should be ok now," she said as I was turning over to lie back down.

"Is my baby going to be alright"? I asked, feeling really scared.

"Everything will be fine. The baby is just moving down into the birth canal and somehow put pressure on the umbilical cord. It's ok now," she said, patting me on my leg.

I was uneasy after that. I couldn't get comfortable. The doctors came in and then left out of the room after they made sure everything was going ok. When I finally settled down an hour or so later, the heart beat stopped again. I called for the nurse again and she repeated what she had done earlier with the code blue.

After the heart beat started back that time, she said, "We're going to have stop your contractions, ok? Something is going on in there and we have to make sure this baby does not lose any more oxygen. I don't know if the umbilical cord is trapped in the crease of the arm or maybe the leg, but if we stop the contractions, hopefully, the baby will move off the cord and everything will be fine."

"I am so scared," I cried as they came and gave me a shot to stop the contractions.

"Just rest, we're going to keep an eye on you, ok? Don't worry," she said.

Why did people say stupid things like that? Of course I was going to worry. I didn't want my baby coming with something wrong with it for lack of oxygen. "Dear Lord, please help my baby," I prayed softly.

♪♪♫♫♪♫♪♫♪

I had already been at the hospital for close to ten hours when I had started to feel sick. Jacob had gone into the waiting room to stretch out. He had called his mother and told her not to come back because there were some problems. As bad as things had been going for us, I knew he didn't want anything to happen to the baby.

When the nurse came in to check my vitals, I asked, "Can I please have some water? I'm so thirsty."

"I'm sorry, I can't give you anything to drink, but I can give you some ice chips."

"I don't care, I need something. I am so hot," I said, feeling feverish.

"I'll be right back," she said, and was back within five minutes with the ice chips. The coldness of the ice felt so good in my throat. "Ok, let me just take a look at you." She lifted the sheet from between my legs and said, "My goodness, you're going to lay right here and have this baby. I can see the top of its head and whatever it is, it's got a head full of hair. We got to get you into the delivery room."

Finally, I said to myself.

"This is it," Jacob said when he got back in the room.

"I know. It seems like I've been pregnant forever. I can't wait to hold it in my arms."

"Well, you will soon," the nurse said. "Let's get you into delivery."

Since the baby's head was practically out, I only had to give three good pushes and it was here. "You have a beautiful little girl," the nurse said on my last push. I smiled at Jacob as I listened for a cry, but I didn't hear one. Instead, the doctors were running around with her.

"What's going on," I asked, trying to raise up. "Jacob, what's going on? Why is she not crying?" I asked again nervously.

"They are cleaning her up, it looks like," he said.

"Nurse, I wanna see my baby," I said anxiously.

"Ok, just a minute," she replied.

I knew something had to be wrong. That didn't happen when Angela had Christopher. Something just wasn't right.

Jacob was about to go over where they were when I heard the most beautiful cry ever. The nurse then brought her over and laid her on my stomach while the doctor finished cleaning me up.

"She is so beautiful," I cried as I looked into her eyes. "She looks just like you, Jacob," I said, looking up at him.

"She does, don't she?" he said, blushing.

"Shanna Nicole is the perfect name for her, isn't it?" I asked.

"Yep. A pretty name for a pretty baby," he grinned.

"I'm going to get her cleaned up and get you into recovery. I'll let you see her a little later," the doctor said.

After they wheeled me into recovery, Jacob left to tell everybody the news. I was mentally exhausted and just wanted to rest.

I had been in the room for only a few minutes when two doctors came into the recovery room. "How are you feeling, Ms. Johnson?" one of them asked.

"Much better now," I said, turning over to look at them.

"Ms. Johnson, my name is Dr. Pearson and I work in neonatal care. Your daughter was born with a temperature of one hundred and two degrees."

"One hundred and two degrees?" I asked, raising up in the bed.

"Yes, ma'am. What we'd like to do is run some tests on her to make sure she doesn't have meningitis. When a baby is born with a temperature of that magnitude, we have to pay special attention to them. What we'd like to do is give her a spinal tap to see if she might have an infection in her brain, but as you know, a spinal tap could cause paralysis. It will take seventy-two hours for the results to come back. Ms. Johnson, we have a sick baby on our hands, and we want to do everything we can to make her better."

Shocked could not describe how I really felt. Why did Jacob have to leave? It was too big a weight to have on my shoulders and I had to make a difficult decision. What would happen if I said no and she never functioned normally? I would have to live with it. What would happen if I said yes, and something went wrong and she never got the opportunity to walk? I would feel guilty every time I saw her in a wheel chair and would never be able to forgive myself. I knew something was wrong. I could feel it. *Lord, why do things always have to be so hard for me?* My head was pounding.

"Give me the paper," I told the doctors. *If something goes wrong, I hope she forgives me,* I said to myself.

♫♪♫♪♫♪♫♪

Sometime during the night, the doctor came in and told me that everything went well. I asked if I could go see her, but he told me to wait until I got to my room, which would be any minute. As soon as I got to my room, I grabbed on to the IV pole I still had attached to me, and started down the hallway to the nursery. I had to brace myself at first because I was still feeling weak from giving birth. When I got to the nursery, I didn't see my baby and became alarmed. I knocked on the window to get the nurse's attention. When she came to the door, I asked, "Where is the Johnson baby?"

"Hey, come in," she said. "Because your baby is so sick, we had to place her in special care. Follow me."

Oh, my God, I said to myself, fighting back tears. She led me to a room behind the nursery and there, sprawled out on one of the tables, was my newborn baby girl. She had monitors placed on her chest and on her back, and had an IV coming out of her little foot. She had scratches on her face and puffy eyes, I knew came from her cries. I looked down at her sleeping face and whispered softly in her ear, "I'm sorry, baby." I bent over and kissed her on the forehead. I grabbed her little hand and kissed it as I looked at her again, lying there sprawled out with only a pamper on. "Can I hold her?" I asked the nurse.

"Yes, you can, but be careful not to get tangled up in her IV. We'd hate to have to stick her again. Here, why don't you try feeding her?" she said, handing me a bottle. "She hasn't eaten yet."

I picked Shanna up and rocked her in my arms. She was so innocent. Why was she subjected to so much pain right at the beginning of her life? As soon as I put the bottle in her mouth, she began to suck. She opened her eyes and looked right at me. She was the most beautiful baby I had ever seen. She had long, curly hair and her skin was so light, you could have mistaken her for white. She had deep, dark eyes and her dad's nose and mouth. I was so happy to finally hold her in my arms, and I could already feel the bond between us growing. I loved her so much, and vowed that if she survived this, I would do everything in my power to give her my best.

After three long, mentally draining days of waiting, all of Shanna's tests results came back negative and I was finally able to take my baby girl home.

Chapter 12

Shanna was such a joy to have in my life. You could never tell she had such a painful beginning. No matter how difficult things were, and they were difficult, she made my life worth living. Jacob still said nothing to me about marriage. Every time I asked him about it, he would change the subject. Shanna and I stayed with my friend, Ramona, a long time friend of the family. She wanted to make sure we were being taken care of so she asked us to come live with her until I got on my feet. I had no idea when that would be, so I was grateful. She lived in a beautiful house. It was clean all the time and there was always something to eat. It was situated in the country and I would take Shanna out on the back porch and push her in her swing for hours. Oh how I wished the house was mine. Jacob would come by every day after work to visit. I was glad to see him at times and other times I resented it. He did not hold up to his end of the bargain. I soon realized that I could not rely on him or his promises. I had to figure out a way to get myself out of this mess.

♫♪♪♫♪♫♪♪

September came and the leaves were beginning to turn bright red, yellow, and orange. I loved the fall. The weather wasn't hot anymore, which gave me and Shanna more time outside. She was a big girl now. She already had a mouth full of teeth and was trying to walk. Everybody kept telling me, "Look out, she's moving out of the way for another one." I made sure that didn't happen. I believe I started taking two birth control pills a day after that.

"Jacob, we are having our family reunion in two weeks. Will you go with me?" I asked him one day during one of his visits.

"I don't want to go to no family reunion. All you see there are a bunch of old people."

"We don't have to stay long, just long enough for everybody to see Shanna. I want them to see how beautiful she is."

"Call yo' sister and see if you can go with her. I ain't going."

"Alright," I said, disappointed. I could see a change in him. He didn't act like he used to. He was beginning to act emotionally detached. I hadn't done anything differently, so I couldn't imagine why he was acting that way. He didn't even come over the next week at all and since I didn't have a car, I couldn't go over to his house to see him.

♫♪♫♪♫♪♫♪♫♪

"Hey, Steven!" I said to Jacob's brother one day in the grocery store. Steven was fine, too. He stood close to six feet and was slightly muscular. He had the same good hair and caramel skin as Jacob. He always dressed nice and was a good catch for any girl.

"Hey, Sara, how you doing? Hey, Shanna, how you doing, girl?" he asked, tickling her under her chin. She let out a big laugh.

"I am doing ok. I haven't seen yo' brother in a week. Is he still at home?"

Steven looked at me pitifully. "Sara, don't tell him I told you this, but he is seeing somebody else."

My heart fell to the floor. "Who?" I asked, hoping it wasn't someone I knew.

"Her name is Leslie and she works at Roses in the mall in the makeup section. He is supposed to be going with her to a wedding next weekend. She ain't even pretty, Sara. She got bucked teeth and a big butt." *So, that's why that motherfucker couldn't go with me to the family reunion.* "I'm sorry, Sara," he said.

"Not as sorry as I am."

"Well, I gotta go. It was good seeing you again, Sara. Bye, little girl," he said as he walked away.

"Thanks, Steven, see ya later." Of course, the tears built up in my eyes again. I tell you, sometimes I get so mad at myself for crying so damn easy. I believe I had over active tear ducts. It was the second time that motherfucker done cheated on me in the year. I guess I wasn't good enough for him no more. *Yeah, motherfucker, ruin my life and leave.*

"Ramona, can I borrow yo' car for about an hour?" I asked when we got back from the store. I was about to pay this girl a visit.

"Yeah, but only for an hour. I got to go to work tonight."

"I'll make sure I'm back in time. I'm taking Shanna with me." I wanted that bitch to see what her new man was about. I bet he didn't tell her he had a family.

"Here," Ramona said, handing me $20.00. "Put some gas in the car for me."

"Alright," I said, grabbing the money and keys at the same time. It would take me about fifteen minutes to get to the mall.

"Please, let her be working today," I said as I strapped Shanna in her car seat.

When I walked over to the makeup section, bingo, she was there. I knew right away who she was. Her teeth stuck out a mile long and her nose looked like Pinocchio's. She did have a big butt, though, which was something I didn't have. I stayed around one hundred twenty five pounds, give or take a few pounds.

"Hi, may I help you?" she asked, grinning, showing all those teeth.

I wanted to say, 'No, but I know a dentist who can help you.' "No, thank you, I'm just looking." I said as she looked at me suspiciously. "Mmm, this smells good. Shanna, do you think your daddy, JACOB, would like this?" I asked, spraying some cologne in the air. She looked up at me, then at Shanna. "Look, Leslie, I know about you and Jacob. I don't know if he told you this, but he has a family. I would appreciate it if you backed off and let us work this out."

"Wow, funny he didn't mention you," she said, sounding surprised.

"Why would he? He was only thinking about 'Mr. Happy.' If he told you about us, that would ruin his chances of making 'Mr. Happy' happy. Listen, I am not here to start no trouble, just to ask you to leave my family alone. Ok? See ya later," I said as I walked away feeling kinda bad for what I had just done. It really wasn't her fault. She was a victim, too, but I wanted to let her know what she was getting herself into.

"Jacob, come over here and get yo' shit!" I demanded on the phone when I was finally able to reach him. He didn't have much, but what little he had, had to go. "You are the sorriest man I have ever met. You will never see Shanna again and if you are not here by 8:00, say goodbye to yo' shit!" I screamed and slammed the phone down. I knew deep down I didn't mean that. I didn't want to raise a kid by myself. I knew I was already doing it anyway, but he was still in the picture. I didn't want to be a statistic and be one of them young girls with a baby and no daddy. I wanted him in the picture somewhere, even though I knew he wasn't shit.

When he arrived he started his plea. "Sara, I'm sorry. I don't know what I was thinking. I don't want to lose you and Shanna. I don't know what I'm going to do now. You don't want me, Leslie called me a compulsive liar and said she never wanted to see me again. I ain't got nobody," he said, really thinking I was going to feel sorry for him. I did.

"So, what you want me to do, feel sorry for you? What about me, Jacob? What about me and my dreams? You didn't have to stay with me. I told you what I wanted to do with my life, you should have let me. You have done none of the things you said you were going to do. When I get myself together, I'm leaving here, Jacob."

"To go where? You ain't got no car, no job. Where you going?"

"Oh, so you think you got the upper hand? You might have it right now, buddy, but not always. Mark my word."

"We'll see," he said, halfway laughing like I was a joke.

"Yeah, we'll see." I went to get his things that I had already bagged up. "Here you go. You can leave now."

"Sara, give me another chance?"

"A chance to do what, Jacob? Make a fool out me again? How many times do you think you can keep doing this and get away with it?"

"I learned my lesson, Sara. I won't do it again."

Lord, why did you make me so weak? I know he is sorry, but he is the daddy of my baby. I don't want her to grow up without him, but I can't keep letting him do this to me. "Alright, Jacob, this is the last time. Do it again and you're out."

"You don't have to worry, baby, I won't," he said, pulling me close to kiss him. I didn't know why he had that power over me, but he did and before I knew it, we were making love right there on the floor. In a way that I couldn't explain, I was glad he stayed.

Chapter 13

"Yeah, girl, Nita told me he been trying to get her to go out with him. I told her you were going with him, but she said he told her he didn't have a girlfriend," Asha told me as I was cleaning the grill at Hardee's a couple of years later. I worked at Hardee's so much you would have thought it was the family business, but hey, at least I was working.

"You know what, Asha? I ain't surprised. He can have whoever he wants. I am so tired of him. He has been cheating on me since day one. He lied and told me he would stay in the military and marry me. Shanna is almost three, do you see a ring on my finger? Hell no," I said, showing her my hand. "He'll get his when the time comes." Of course, he denied Nita, too.

♫♪♫♪♫♪♫♪♫

I was finally able to move into my very own place. Ramona helped me find it when I got a job paying a little bit more money. It wasn't a mansion, but it was still a nice place. It had two big bedrooms and one bathroom. I was glad I was able to give Shanna her own room. It had a big kitchen and a nice sized living room. It was just enough room for the two of us. Ramona gave me furniture for it and I fixed it up nicely. It wasn't too bad for my first place. You probably wondering why Jacob didn't find us a place, ain't you? Me too, sorry joker.

JaLisa and I had gotten a job at the local factory. It wasn't a place I wanted to work forever, but it paid me enough to take good care of Shanna. A lady down the road kept her for me and I dropped her off every morning on the way to work. I still didn't have a car so I rode with JaLisa until she got a better job and left.

When JaLisa stopped working there, the company van picked me up in the mornings and dropped me off in the evenings. In the evenings when I was dropped off to pick Shanna up, I would walk home from there. I had to walk down the road about a mile in temperatures of ninety plus degrees in grass as high as my knees with her on my hip. Since it was on the main road, there was constant traffic. Nothing was more humiliating to me. The sad part about it was Jacob knew it, but did nothing to help. When I got home every day, I would take Shanna into the bathroom and pick ticks off of her, and then off me. One day she came into the living room and said, "Here, Mommy, you forgot one," holding her thumb and forefinger together with a tick in between them.

I took it from her, burned it, and said, "One day, it's gonna get better, baby, ok? I promise you."

"Ok, Mommy," she said. I took her and squeezed her to me. I shook my head in disbelief as I realized what my life had come to.

♫♪♫♪♫♪♫♪♫

Even though Jacob only lived ten minutes away, he only stopped by during the weekends. That was just to have sex, but I would do it just to keep him coming around.

"Suck it, Sara?" he asked one day.

"What?" I snapped. I just had a flashback. *"Suck it,"* Richard had said. *"Put it in yo' mouth and suck it now."* I didn't want to remember that day. I didn't want to remember him. Jacob had never asked me to do that before. "Jacob, I don't know how. I never did that before."

"It is easy. All you have to do is put it in your mouth and suck it. Do a little bit at a time."

I looked at it, and then I looked at him. "Jacob, I can't. I'm sorry, but I just can't."

"Don't worry about it, Sara. If you don't want to do it, it won't be no problem finding someone who will," he said as he got up and started to get dressed.

"Ok, I'll do it," I said, hoping it would make him stay longer.

"That's more like it," he said, getting back in the bed.

I slowly moved down to his dick. I looked at it, closed my eyes, and took a deep breath. *Here goes,* I said to myself. I stuck my tongue out just enough to taste it. I slowly put my whole mouth around the head. I was starting to get sick. I tasted it a little more until I had it touching the back of my mouth. I gagged and took my mouth off of it. I looked at him and looked back at his dick. I braced myself as I tried it again. I did the same thing.

"Get up, Sara," he scolded like I could have been Shanna. "You are pathetic. Let me up."

"No, Jacob, let me try again," I pleaded. I put it back in my mouth. That time, I put it all the way in my mouth, but then I smelled something. It smelled like straight up ass. I gagged, took it out of my mouth, and didn't care how mad he got. He had a nerve to ask me to suck his dick and he hadn't even washed his nasty ass.

Jacob got up, got his clothes on, and said, "I'll see you next time," and walked out the door. At that point, I didn't care if he never came back. I wasn't gon' be sucking no stinking ass dick.

♫♪♫♪♫♪♫♪

Shanna had just celebrated her third birthday and let me tell you, that girl was smart. She started doing everything early. She got her first tooth at three months and started walking at seven months. Now, at the age of three, she was reading like she was already in school, mostly from memorization. She read the same little book over and over again. Whenever anyone asked her to read them a story, she would go get that book. She would impress them every time, but I knew her secret. I was proud of my little girl though. We spent so much time together. I tried to make up for the time her daddy didn't spend with her. I swear that girl had a big vocabulary. She could actually hold a conversation. I was glad I had her to keep me company. No matter how badly things were going in my life, she was one thing I knew I did right.

Some months had gone by and one morning I woke up and felt so dizzy I thought I was going to pass out. It had been happening off and on for several days, but that day was the worst. I went to the doctor's office and was not at all surprised by the news.

"You're what?" Jacob screamed at me and drew back like he wanted to hit me.

"I'm pregnant!" I said to him again boldly. Did I want to be? Hell no. But, what would it hurt? My life was going nowhere fast anyway. It wasn't like I had a promising future. He had already taken that from me.

"That baby ain't mine and if you have it, I'm leaving."

"Why do you say that now, Jacob, huh? Why in the hell didn't you say that three years ago and I wouldn't be here in your life while you go around and treat me like a dog. I'm going to have this baby whether you like it or not. So, if you are leaving, you better get going."

"You know what? You ain't shit," he said. "I don't want you and nobody else will, either. Look at you. How much you weigh, ninety pounds? You ain't the prettiest thang I ever saw and now you got *two* youngins? Who gonna want you? I sure as hell don't, so go ahead and have yo' babies. I'm moving to Jacksonville. See you when I see you, and that will be too soon."

"Stop yelling at my mama!" Shanna screamed with tears running down her face. I was so caught up in him that I didn't realize that she was standing there.

"Get out of my house!" I warned. He looked at me and then at Shanna, who I had run and picked up. He didn't say a word, just turned around and left. "It's going to be ok, baby. It's going to be ok."

♫♪♫♪♫♪♫♪

I continued to work at the factory because I needed to work more than ever. I would soon have another mouth to feed. I walked with my head down most of the time and I had absolutely no self esteem at all. It was true what I had heard all my life. I was just an ugly, nappy headed girl. Two kids, no car, and a job I didn't want to work at forever, but was glad I had it. I had no reason to hold my head up.

"Hey, how are you?" Sam asked one day from across the assembly line.

"Fine," I said reluctantly. I wasn't trying to have a conversation with anybody. I had noticed him looking at me all week, but he never said anything and neither did I.

"What's the matter? Why do you always look so sad?"

"'Cause, motherfucker, I ain't got nothing to be happy about,' I wanted to say. "Because my mama is an alcoholic," was the best I could give him.

"Oh! I'm sorry to hear that," he said and nothing else. I was glad he left me the hell alone.

The next morning when I went to clock in, I heard someone call me from behind. I turned around to see Sam standing there with some brochures in his hands on alcoholism. "I hope these help."

I looked up at him and shook my head. "Thank you," I said, taking the brochures.

"It would be good to see you smile every now and then," he said, smiling.

"Well, first you got to give me something to smile about," I said, still trying to avoid a conversation.

"I'm sure there is plenty to smile about. What you have to do is stop concentrating on all the bad."

"How do you know what I'm concentrating on?" I asked, annoyed.

"The way you're walking around looking, it can't be good."

I sucked my teeth and walked away. Sam had smooth, chocolate skin with slightly thick lips. He wore wire rimmed spectacles and had his head shaved bald. He had a pleasant smile and talked like he was from upstate somewhere. He had a nice build, like he worked out a lot. He wasn't chiseled, but still looked fit and stood about five feet ten. As the day went on, we talked more and he wasn't such a bad person to talk to after all.

When I went in the next morning, I was kinda looking forward to talking to him. We worked side by side that day and he did make me smile from time to time. "Sam, my mama is not an alcoholic. She drinks a little excessively sometimes, but that was not the reason I held my head down. I have been dating this guy for a few years and I am now pregnant with his second child. He told me if I had the baby, he would leave me. He did and I haven't heard from him in weeks."

"You know what? When you see him again, you tell him you found a man to be the father to your baby." And from the expression on his face, I believed him. We continued to talk and I was really beginning to like him. "Why don't you let me come by and see you?" he asked.

"I don't know, Sam. I got a lot going on."

"Look, I like you, ok? I like you a lot. You have qualities any good man would appreciate. I won't stay long, I promise. How about it?"

"Ok, I think I'd like that," I relented.

Sam came by about 7:00 and I had taken out the game of *Monopoly* for us to play. We could have watched a movie, but I wanted to interact with him to see where his head was.

"Ok, that's it. You're bankrupt," I said, taking his last house.

"Man, I give," he said, pulling back from the table. "I'm glad this is only a game. I'd be in the poor house dealing with you."

"Yes, you would," I said, teasing. "I tried to give you a break, but lady luck wasn't on your side."

"I'll get you next time," he said confidently. "Ok, lady. I said I wouldn't stay long, so I better get going," Sam said, getting up. "I had a nice time."

"I did, too," I said as I got up to walk him to the door. Before he opened it, he turned and gave me a hug. When he bent down to kiss me, my body wanted more. As much as I wanted him to stay, I let him leave.

Chapter 14

Sam and I continued to see each other and, believe it or not, I looked forward to going to work. We worked close together almost every day. He came by the house almost every weekend and he definitely knew how to put it down in the bedroom. Jacob still hadn't come by, but I didn't miss him. I was glad he wasn't bothering me anymore. Shanna asked about him from time to time and I'd tell her he'd be back soon.

"Sam, what are you doing for Thanksgiving?" I asked. Thanksgiving was only a couple of weeks away.

"Why, are you inviting me over?" he asked, looking like he was hoping that I was.

"Yeah, I think it would be nice to have you over. This will be the first Thanksgiving in my house and I think you would be great company," I said, smiling at him, hoping he'd say yes.

"I'd love to come. Just tell me what time."

"Alright, don't stand me up now."

"You can best believe I wouldn't miss this for the world."

♫♪♫♪♫♪♫♪

The next morning started off pretty rough. I woke up throwing up. That was the worst part about being pregnant, the morning sickness. I still had a long way to go. The baby wasn't due 'til June. I couldn't wait to get past that first trimester. I didn't feel like going to work, so I stayed home in the bed. I was sure Shanna didn't mind, she got to sleep in. Everything I ate came right back up. I kept crackers on the night stand and ate them to keep from being hungry. Around 12:00, someone knocked on the door. *How does anybody know I'm home?* I wondered. I was not going to answer it.

"Do you want me to get the door, Mommy?" Shanna asked from inside her room where she was playing with her dolls.

"No, baby, I'll get it." Before I could get up, they knocked again. I knew if I didn't answer it they were going to continue to knock, so I drug myself to the door. "Who is it?" I managed to say. My stomach was so sore from throwing up so much.

"It's me, baby, Sam. Are you ok?"

"Yeah," I said, unlocking the door. "What are you doing here?" I asked as I attempted to comb my hair back with my fingers. I knew I looked like shit but at that particular moment, I didn't care.

"I came by to check on you. When you didn't come to work, I got worried about you."

"I'm ok, morning sickness just kicking my ass. Did you eat lunch? I can make you a sandwich if you want me to."

"You go back and lie down and get some rest. Don't worry about me." I made my way back to my bed with him dead on my heels.

"Do you want me to get you something?"

"No, I'm ok."

"I can stay here if you want me to."

"No, you go back to work. Call me later."

"Ok. Shanna, you take care of Mommy, ok?"

"Ok," she said, not even looking up from her dolls.

"I'll let myself out."

"Ok, see you later." I managed to smile.

I had been asleep for a couple of hours when someone knocked on the door again. That time, Shanna was asleep at the foot of the bed. I got up quietly to keep from waking her. When she didn't get her nap out, she was cranky as hell. *Who in the hell is it now?* I asked myself. I looked at the kitchen clock and it was a little after five.

"Who is it?" I asked quietly.

"It's Jacob, open the door."

Who in the hell did he think he was demanding me to open *my* door? I hadn't seen him in weeks. "What do you want, Jacob?" I asked through the closed door.

"I came to see Shanna. Open the door."

"She's asleep. Come back another time."

"You got somebody in there, Sara?" By that time, I heard Shanna crying from the room.

"Ugh!" I knew I was in for a long night. I opened the door and let him in. I didn't want to, but Shanna had been asking about him.

"You look like shit," he said, sitting down on *my* couch. "Come here, Shanna." She went over and sat on his lap. "How you been doing?" he asked her.

"Fine," she whined. She looked at me and said, "Mommie, I want some water."

"Come and get it, baby," I said from the kitchen.

"So, Sara, how yo' pregnancy coming along?" he asked like he was hoping I wasn't pregnant anymore.

"Fine, and you don't have to worry. I found somebody to be the father of my baby," I responded proudly.

"Is that right? Let's see how long he sticks around." I didn't say nothing. I wasn't in the mood. I had been sick all day and I was not about to get into it with him, so I let that one slide.

"Shanna, go over there and talk to yo' daddy so he can leave."

"Why, expecting someone?"

"Jacob, will you please go? I am not feeling well."

"Yeah, Sara, I'll go. I'll come back when you're feeling better, in about seven months," he said sarcastically. He gave Shanna a hug and left.

♫♪♫♪♫♪♫♪

I was glad it was a short week. I could not wait for Thursday to come. "Do we still have a date for Thursday?" I asked Sam when I got to work on Monday.

"You bet," he said, smiling. "Do you feel better?"

"Much better. I can't wait to get to my second trimester. I got another month to go."

"You look great."

"Thank you," I said, wanting to believe him. We talked for the rest of the day and he had me smiling all the time. I couldn't wait to cook for him. I wasn't that good of a cook, but I was going to do my best.

It was finally Thanksgiving Day. I was so excited to see Sam. When I heard the knock on the door, I knew it had to be him. "Coming!" I yelled, wiping my hands on my apron as I opened the door. "Hey, come on in."

"Happy Thanksgiving!" he said, giving me a hug. He didn't kiss me in front of Shanna.

"Happy Thanksgiving to you. Come on in and make yourself comfortable. Let me take your coat. I am almost finished."

"It smells good up in here."

"Thanks. I hope it tastes as good as it smells. The remote is on the table. I think the game is on."

Sam watched the game until I called him in for dinner. "You don't have to tell me twice," he said, coming into the kitchen.

"Come on, Shanna, you sit right here," I said, lifting her into her booster seat. We said grace and started eating.

"Sara, that was great. Where did you learn to cook like that?" he asked, finishing off his pumpkin pie.

"I don't know, I guess from my mama. She has always been a good cook. I don't cook much since it's just me and Shanna. I got lucky this time. Shanna, do you want something else to eat?" I asked as she sat at the table looking from me to Sam.

"No, ma'am. Can I go look at TV?"

"Sure, you can," I said as I helped her from the table.

"I am going to watch the *Smurfs.*"

"Ok, I'll be in there shortly," I assured her. "Thank you so much for coming, Sam," I said when I sat back down at the table. "I am really enjoying this day."

"Me too," he said putting his hand on mine. "I am glad you invited me."

I was startled by another knock on the door. "Who in the world keep knocking on my door?" I asked, annoyed as I got up to answer it.

"I don't know," Sam said.

"Who is it?" I yelled.

"It's Jacob." My heart skipped a beat and I began to shake nervously. For some reason, I felt like I had done something wrong. I looked at Sam who was sitting there so calm.

"Let him in," he said as gently as he could.

I opened the door and Jacob came in looking like the cat that had just swallowed the canary.

"What's up?" he asked Sam as he took a seat at the kitchen table where we were sitting. I had never felt so uncomfortable in my life. There I was sitting at the table with my new lover and the daddy of my babies. What a position to be put in.

"Sam, this is Jacob. Jacob, this is Sam," I said awkwardly. They both looked at each other, but neither one of them said a word.

"Did Sara tell you she was pregnant?" Jacob asked.

"Yeah, she told me. She also told me you left her."

"Yeah, well, I been thinking about that. I think maybe I ought to come back and take care of 'em."

I almost choked on my tongue. *Take care of us? He had never taken care of us.*

"Oh yeah? What do you have to say about that, Sara?" Sam asked. I was speechless. There we were having a wonderful Thanksgiving dinner and here comes Jacob messing everything up like he always did.

"Well, Sara?" Jacob asked like he was enjoying himself.

"I don't know," was all I managed to get out.

"You don't know?" Sam asked, confused. *What in the world was I saying?*

"Sara, you know I care about you. We already got one kid and are about to have another one. I want to be here for my family. I don't think I could live without ya'll."

"Well, you managed to do just fine these last couple of months."

"No, I didn't. I wanted to come back ever since I left, I just didn't know how to ask. Today I finally got up the courage and here I am. I missed you and Shanna so much. I know I said some harsh things and I'm sorry. I just want to be with my family. I promise I will do better. What do you say? Can I come back?"

"Wait a minute, I think I got to throw up."

I left the kitchen and ran to the bathroom. I threw up everything I just ate, then some of yesterday's food, too. The day was going too good. I should have known something was going to mess it up, namely Jacob. *What you gonna do, Sara? I asked myself. Sam has always treated you good, but Jacob started out that way, too, look how he turned out. You do have a family with Jacob. I do want to keep my family together, but I love Sam. I have to go out there and say something and somebody is not going to like what I have to say, especially me.*

"Ok," I said as I sat back down to the table. "Jacob, you know you are a low down dirty dog and have always treated me like shit, and, Sam, you have been absolutely wonderful to me, but I don't think I can love you completely as long as Jacob is around and I never want to hurt you. You have meant so much to me, but I have to look past me and do what I think is best for my family, so as much as I hate to, I guess I'll take Jacob back." I immediately saw the pain on his face. "Not for me, Sam, but for the family."

He looked at me for a long, long time. The look on his face was, 'Why? Why would you stay with a man who treats you this way?' But, he didn't say a word. He got up from the table, asked for his coat, and waited by the door while I went to get it. When I came back, tears were rolling down my face.

"I'm sorry, Sam," I managed to say.

"Feel my chest, Sara." He took my hand and put it on his heart. "You feel that?"

"Yes, your heart?"

"Yeah, you just broke it." He bent down, kissed me on the lips, and walked out the door.

When I closed the door, I leaned on it and cried for a couple of minutes. I turned around and looked at Jacob. "I hate you," I screamed, and ran into my room.

Chapter 15

Over the next several months, Jacob did try and make a difference. He came by pretty regularly and Shanna loved it when he played house with her. I still could not get over how I hurt Sam. When I went back to work the week after Thanksgiving, he was gone. I felt such a void that I got another job, too, because working at the factory was unbearable. There were too many memories.

I was seven months pregnant and Jacob still hadn't taken me to see his family. For whatever reason, he was ashamed and I didn't understand why. I didn't get too big during my pregnancies, and most people could not believe I was as far along as I was. So, I wasn't at all surprised when I got that same reaction from his mama.

"Well, Sara, you looking forward to this baby?" Lucy asked one Sunday afternoon after Jacob finally took me over to his house for dinner.

"Yes, ma'am. I am ready to give Shanna somebody to play with."

"Is that right? So, you are having this baby for Shanna?"

I wanted to throw the mashed potatoes I had on my spoon and hit her dead between the eyes. "No, ma'am. I am having the baby because I got pregnant. It will be good for Shanna to have somebody to play with is what I was trying to say," I said, annoyed.

"Well, we got to go shopping and buy you some maternity clothes. You starting to show and those clothes you got on look a little snug. How far along are ya?"

"Seven months."

"Seven months?" she said with much surprise. "Jacob, we ain't gon' have time to go shopping then. Shoot, she gonna have that baby before you know it. I thought you just got pregnant," she said, turning back to me.

"No, ma'am. I guess Jacob just decided not to tell you," I said, looking at him disgusted.

"Well, if you need something just let me know. I want to make sure you got what you need for the baby."

"Thank you. I will."

"Shanna, you ready to be a big sister?" she asked.

"Yes, ma'am," Shanna said, shoving peas in her mouth.

"You gon' be one soon," she continued.

"I know. Mama got a baby in her stomach. It's gonna come out soon, then I'm gone have somebody to play my dolls with."

"Good. I know that will be fun." I was so glad when Jacob asked me if I was ready to go. I couldn't wait to get out of there. The air was stifling.

♫♪♫♪♫♪♫♪

One afternoon, I was cleaning the house and I bent down to pick up my niece, Cheyenne, when I heard a thug sound come from between my legs. Before I knew it, water was gushing everywhere.

Cheyenne was Angela's second child. Angela met and married her husband, Rick, right after she had Christopher and later gave birth to Cheyenne. She was there helping me with Shanna and with cleaning the house before the baby came.

"Angela?" I yelled to the back of the apartment I had just moved into. "Angela, I think my water just broke," I yelled again.

She came into the room, looked down at my legs, and said, "Let's go."

We had dropped Shanna, Cheyenne, and Christopher off at Mama's. Angela would be leaving to pick them up as soon as Jacob got to the hospital. I called him and told him to meet me there.

When I got to the hospital, they told me to undress so they could examine me. As soon as the doctor put his fingers inside me, he said to the nurse, "Admit her. She's ready." That was when I felt my first contraction.

"Doctor Mitchell, will you please give me an epidural?"

"Yes. I can give you one," he said, then ran down the risks.

"Yes, I know. I had one before with my first child," I said, wanting him to rush and give me the shot.

"Ok, I'll be right back," he said.

Angela held my hand while Dr. Mitchell stuck me in my back. After that, I didn't feel another contraction. Jacob arrived some two and a half hours later, so Angela left to go pick up the kids.

"Where have you been, Jacob? What took you so long to get here?"

"They just now let me off, Sara. I got here as soon as I could. What did the doctor say?"

"He said I will be having the baby any time. I am dilating pretty well, but it is hard to tell exactly when the baby will come. I'm really scared, Jacob. All I can think about is what happened with Shanna. I pray nothing happens to this baby."

"You can't think like that. Everything is going to be fine," he assured me.

Throughout the night, the doctors came in and out, but I wasn't dilated enough to deliver.

"I'm going right outside to the lobby and stretch out for a while," Jacob said. "When the time comes, tell them to come get me."

"Ok," I said and turned over to try and get some sleep.

Thirty minutes later, Dr. Williams came in, checked me, and said, "It's time." He had taken over for Dr. Mitchell.

Lord, please don't let me go through what I went through with Shanna. Please let this be a healthy baby, I said to myself. "Will you go to the lobby and get my boyfriend?" I asked him.

"I sure will. Nurse, get her ready for delivery." He came back in and said, "I'm sorry, ma'am, but I don't see your boyfriend. There is nobody in the lobby."

"You got to be kidding. Will you check again?"

"Yes, ma'am, as soon as we get done prepping you."

When they wheeled me into delivery some fifteen minutes later, the nurse came back in and said, "He is still not out there and we can't wait any longer."

I could not believe he left me all alone, knowing how afraid I was. He was definitely a piece of work. I didn't know where he went or what he did, but when I saw him again, I showed him his new son, Jaylen. Thank God, there were no complications that time.

Chapter 16

I was working third shift on yet another job when I had Jaylen, and it was hard trying to take care of a new baby and trying to work at night. I got absolutely no sleep at all. I eventually quit and went back to the factory, but because the factory didn't pay as much as my third shift job, I had to take on a second job at Burger King in order to make ends meet. My sister, Vanessa, would come by after school and watch the kids in the evenings. Jacob had left me again, that time going to Detroit, chasing some pipe dream. He did leave me his car, though. That was the least he could do considering I had to take care of two kids by myself.

It had been a couple of years of me maintaining. "I got to move," I told JaLisa one day. "I can't keep doing this. I never get to see the kids anymore. Jaylen ain't even gonna know who I am. I don't know how much longer I can keep this up. I feel like I have abandoned them."

"No, you haven't. You are doing the best you can. Maybe Jacob will send you some money soon and you'll be able to quit that second job."

"JaLisa, I am only twenty-four years old. I feel like I am fifty. Life has not dealt me a fair hand. I am too young to have this many burdens. When do I get a break?"

"I don't know, Sara, but if you keep on doing what you're doing, one day you're going to look back and feel so proud of yourself. Look at you. You are out here every day trying to do the best you can for these kids when you could have easily sat at home and drawn welfare. You chose not to, so at least feel proud of yourself for that. Your time is going to come."

"I sure do hope so," I said, laying my head on her shoulder.

♫♪♫♪♫♪♫♪

After the rent went up again another twenty dollars, fifty in the last year, I was forced to move. I could no longer afford it. I moved into a house a little further down the road. Jacob had since moved back and moved in with me. I didn't like the house at all because it was older and the plumbing was messed up. It was dark, damp, and musty smelling, and the carpet had stains everywhere and looked like it needed to be cleaned. The walls were layered with dark paneling and the kitchen floor tile was cracked and curling, but that was the only place available at the time. I had just signed a one year lease, so I had to tough it out. The rent was a lot cheaper, so I was able to quit working at BK. Jacob had also gotten a job, although I couldn't tell when it came to paying bills. One thing I always did was pay my bills.

One Friday evening, I came home from work to find that the lights had been cut off. It was in the middle of summer and there was no way we could stay in that house with no AC. "Jacob, what in the world happened?" I screamed at him when he walked through the door. "Why are the fucking lights cut off? I gave you the money last week to pay the bill. Why are the damn lights off and of all days, today? There is no fucking way we can get them turned back on until Monday, so what are we going to do?"

"Sara, I thought I could make more money off the money you gave me. This dude told me he would buy a gun from me for more than what you gave me, so I went to the pawn shop and bought the gun, but I could not find the guy nowhere."

"Jacob, I gave you money to pay the light bill and you took it to buy a fucking gun? So, you got a gun and no money, and we ain't got no damn lights? Look at these kids. How are we going to eat, huh?"

"Well, I can go to Mama's."

"You can go to yo' mama's, right? What about us, Jacob? What about me, Shanna, and Jaylen? Where we going?"

"Can't you go to yo' mama's?" he asked.

I reached over and slapped him. I could not believe I just did that. I had been angry with him numerous times before, but that time he not only hurt me, but he hurt Shanna and Jaylen, too. It wasn't even his damn money, it was mine. I could not forgive him for that. I guess I deserved it though. I could have been with Sam, but nooo, I chose to stay with that sorry asshole. I went in the back and packed a bag for me and the kids. I didn't know where we were going, but we were getting the hell out of there.

♫♪♫♪♫♪♫♪

There was a new plant opening in the next town over. It was about a twenty five minute drive, but the starting pay was much better than what I was currently making. I had finally saved up enough money to get a cheap car. It took me twenty four years to do it, but it felt good knowing I didn't have to depend on nobody. I was hired at the plant and was made supervisor since I had previous experience. It wasn't long before a tall, pecan colored man caught my eye. He had a slender build and stood close to six feet. When he walked, he looked like he floated.

"Who is that?" I asked Ellen, a girl who was working beside me.

"Oh, that's Brian. He works on the other side of the plant."

"He sho' do look good."

"I know. He fine as hell. He hangs out at my mama's sometimes after work. He is a pretty decent man."

"Is he married?"

"Yeah, but that ain't never stopped nothing. He used to go with Tameka Reeves who works with him on the other side, but they broke up now."

"Oh, he still look good."

Working there made me see myself in a completely different way. Every man that came into that plant to work tried to talk to me. I wondered why, though. Wasn't I the same nappy headed girl I had been called all my life? I think the years must have been good to me. I wasn't ugly at all anymore. I was starting to wonder if I ever really was. I didn't know who came up with, 'sticks and stones may break yo' bones, but words will never hurt you,' but that was a lie straight from Hell. Words had hurt me all my life, and I believed I was what everybody called me. Nothing.

"Hey, how are you?" Brian asked, breaking into my thoughts.

"I'm pretty good, and you?"

"Not too bad. My name is Brian and I saw you from a distance a few days ago, and thought I'd come over and introduce myself."

"I'm Sara, and I'm pleased to meet you." I replied.

"You are a nice looking lady and I was wondering if you would like to go out to dinner sometime."

"Oh yeah? Um, I think I might be able do that," I said, caring less about his marriage. I was miserable with Jacob and I wasn't going to let the opportunity pass me by.

"How about this weekend?" he asked.

"Ah, ok. Where do you have in mind?"

"Let's see. Can you meet me at Grady's on Main Street at 7:00 on Saturday?"

"7:00 it is. Just make sure your wife ain't there," I said, letting him know that I knew he was married.

"You don't have to worry about that. See you then."

"Ok, talk to you later." As soon as I saw Ellen I said, "Ellen, come here, girl. Brian just asked me out. Out of all the women in here, he asked me."

"Why wouldn't he? You the prettiest girl in here."

I could not believe my ears. *Me, pretty? Ain't nobody ever called me pretty.* When I looked around at all the men and how they were checking me out, I asked myself, *Is it possible? Can I be pretty?* No way. It would all turn out to be a joke and I wasn't falling for it.

Chapter 17

"Thank you for watching the kids, JaLisa. I won't be out too late."

"No problem, girl. Have fun!"

I gave Shanna and Jaylen a kiss and ran to the car. I was so excited about my date. Yes, I knew I was still living with Jacob, but I didn't care about him anymore. He was out doing his thang every weekend, so that night, I was out doing mine. I wasn't thrilled about the fact that Brian was married, but I was tired of staying in that house every weekend doing nothing but taking care of the kids and being insulted by Jacob. Don't ask me why I was still with him, 'cause Lord knows I didn't know. My life had been completely miserable ever since he came into it almost ten years ago, but when you had kids by someone, it was hard to break that bond. I guess I wanted him around for their sake. I didn't want them to grow up without a daddy.

"Grady's, Grady's, oh there it is," I said as I rode down Main Street. I had never been there before so I didn't quite know where it was. When I pulled into the parking lot, I saw Brian waiting for me.

"Hey there," he said as he came around to open my door.

Wow, he opened my door. That is a first. He looked so damn good. He had just gotten his hair neatly trimmed and he wore a Polo shirt with tan slacks. I didn't know what the name of his cologne was, but it smelled so good my panties were starting to get wet. Brian was twelve years my senior, but you couldn't tell by looking at him. He looked fine as hell to be close to forty.

"Hey, you look great," I said, admiring him from head to toe.

"You look good yourself. Are you ready to go in?"

"Uh huh." The restaurant was kinda crowded but it *was* Saturday night. Their specialty was seafood. Brian asked the waiter if he could get us a table in the back. I guess that was in case somebody walked in he didn't want to see us.

"What would you like?" he asked me once we were seated and the waiter had given us the menus.

"I think I want the all you can eat crab legs. What about you?"

"I don't know, I think I'll get the shrimp." We gave the waiter our order and waited for our drinks. "So, miss lady, how do you like working at Jackson's?"

"I do. I didn't think I would at first, but it is ok. I'm glad they added the new addition to the plant. I like the hours and the pay is not too bad, either. How long have you been working there?"

"About twenty years."

"Wow, I was in elementary school twenty years ago." I quickly added, "Oops, sorry." I said, slightly embarrassed.

"For what? I guess I'm considerably older than you. How old are you?"

"Twenty-six. Yeah, you robbing the cradle," I said to him, teasing.

"I guess I am. Sara?" he asked. "Have you ever been anywhere else?"

"Not really," I said, trying to forget my visit to Chicago. "What about you?"

"I've visited places, but wouldn't want to live anywhere else but here."

"Well, I'm glad you like it here 'cause I don't. Never have. I just ended up getting stuck here."

"Why is that?"

"It's a long story. I'll tell you about it one of these days."

"Ok. Here comes our food." We continued to talk as we ate our food. When we were done and the waiter brought us the check, I reached inside my pocket book to get the money to pay for my meal. "What are you doing?" he asked.

"I'm paying for my meal."

"I got this," he said, pushing my money away. "I invited you out, remember?"

"Yeah, but this wouldn't be the first time I've been invited out but ended up picking up the tab."

"Not tonight," he said as I put my money away.

"Thank you for inviting me out," I said as we were leaving the restaurant.

"I had a nice time."

"Me too," I said, looking into his eyes, hoping he would kiss me. He reached down and opened my door. He gave me a hug and I got into the car. As I was about to turn on the ignition, he bent over and gave me a kiss.

"See you Monday," he said as he stood up.

"Ok. Have a good night." I backed up my Nissan and waved at him as I drove off.

♩♪♫♪♫♪♫♪♫

"How was it?" JaLisa asked when I went in to pick up the kids.

"I had a great time. Dinner was wonderful."

"I'm glad, 'cause Jacob came over here looking for you."

"Oh really? What did you tell him?"

"I told him you went out with some friends and would be back after awhile. He took the kids with him. I hope he don't start nothing when you get home."

"You know what? I don't care if he does. I am 'bout to leave his ass, anyway. I am tired of living like this. I don't know when, but I'm leaving him."

"Well, it's about damn time. You should have left his sorry ass a long time ago."

"To do what, JaLisa? Bring different men in and out of the kids' lives? Naw. I ain't gon' do that to them."

"Nobody said you had to do that, Sara, but he ain't doing nothing but holding you down."

"You don't think I know that? I have known that for several long years, but all that is 'bout to change. I am leaving his ass just as soon as I get on my feet. Thanks for watching the kids."

"Anytime, they are good kids. See ya."

"Bye." We hugged and I left.

♩♪♫♪♫♪♫♪♫

"Where the hell you been?" Jacob yelled as soon as I got in the house.

"Where the hell you been?" I snapped back.

"I been here waiting for yo' ass."

"What happened, you got stood up tonight?"

"Stood up from what, Sara? How many times you gon' keep accusing me?"

"As many times as you keep going out there fucking around. You must think you got me wrapped around yo' finger, well, you don't. I am sick and tired of yo' shit. You don't do nothing 'round here but eat, sleep, and make a fucking mess for me to clean up. Look at this place, fucking clothes everywhere. I thought you said you were going to do the laundry. There are dirty dishes in the sink after I just finished washing them and you wonder why we got roaches. How many times I got to tell yo' ass not to eat in the living room? You sorry, you trifling, and I am fed up with yo' sorry ass."

"So, what you gon' do, leave me again? How many times you done said that, Sara? A hundred, a thousand? You ain't going nowhere, you know why? 'Cause don't nobody else want you. You lucky I'm still here.

"I hate you, Jacob. I fucking hate you."

"Um, I fucking love you, too." He got up and walked out the front door. I looked over and grabbed a vase off the coffee table, opened the door, and threw it at him.

"Don't you fucking come back!" I screamed. The vase caught him on his elbow.

"Are you crazy?" he yelled, turning around.

"Yes, I'm crazy. Crazy for putting up with yo' trifling ass. You know ain't nobody else gon' put up wit' it, that's why you keep coming back to me. Yes. I am crazy," I said, and went back in the house and slammed the door. I heard him crank up the car and leave. I was glad with all the yelling that went on, the kids stayed asleep. Yet again, he ruined another perfectly good night. I hoped Brian didn't have to go through the same thing when he got home.

♫♪♫♪♫♪♫♪♫

I did finally leave Jacob when my lease was up. I moved to a local trailer park and Jacob moved back home with his mama, *again*. Brian and I continued to see each other over the next couple of years. He did a lot for me. He helped me pay a bill or two from time to time, we always went out to eat, but we always had to go out of town. We used to go fishing after work when we got off early enough and I always enjoyed his company. He would even come cut my grass when Jacob's sorry ass wouldn't. One time it got so high, I couldn't even find Jaylen.

"Did your wife come back yet?" I asked him one day on the fishing bank.

"No, she ain't back." They had recently separated and I had nothing to do with it. I didn't know how we did it, but she never found out about our relationship. I didn't put any pressure on him because I didn't want to be responsible for breaking up no marriage. I never expected him to be mine, anyway. I just enjoyed his company. I was getting tired of sneaking around though. I missed him during holidays and I hated the fact that he never spent the night. That was probably a good thing though with that crazy ass Jacob living close by.

After a while, money started getting tight again. It seemed like every time I turned around, I had to put the car in the shop. I came home one day and found a notice on the door saying they were about to cut off my lights. After Jacob refused to help, I had to ask Brian for the money. I wasn't 'bout to let my lights get cut off again. Every time I asked Jacob for help he came up with an excuse, so I did what I had to do.

"Jacob, if you don't start giving me money for these kids, I'm going to take you to court," I told him one day when I hardly had enough money for Shanna's lunch.

"I been giving you money," he said lamely.

"What's twenty-five dollars a week, Jacob? Shanna needs money for school and I got to pay a babysitter for Jaylen. That little money you giving me ain't enough. I can't do this by myself."

"Well, that's all I'm giving you and you better be glad you getting that."

"You know what, Jacob, I'm tired of begging you. I'm taking yo' ass to court."

"Go ahead. I bet I won't have to pay what you asking for."

"Ok, count it as done. I'll see you in court."

♫♪♫♪♫♪♫♪

"In the case of Johnson vs. Thompson, will the party please come forward?" the magistrate asked when it was our day in court. Jacob and I made our way to the front of the courtroom. Of course, he brought his mama.

"Mr. Thompson, do you work?"

"Yes, Your Honor. I work for Sonny's Moving Co."

"Do you have a copy of your check stub?"

"Yes, Your Honor."

"Bring that to me," he ordered one of the police officers.

"Miss Johnson, does Mr. Thompson give you any money for support?"

"Your Honor, he gives me a different amount a week, never exceeding $100.00 a month."

"Mr. Thompson, do you think that is enough to support your two children?"

"Yes, Your Honor."

"I disagree. Miss Johnson, how much money do you think you need to care for these children?"

"I need at least $300.00 dollars a month, Your Honor."

"Mr. Thompson, you are ordered this day to pay $350.00 a month child support to the plaintiff. Do you understand?"

"I understand, Your Honor."

"Good, now get out of this courtroom."

♫♪♫♪♫♪♫♪♫

"Girl, I feel so much better," I told JaLisa when I got home that afternoon. "I can't believe he thought $100.00 a month was enough. I told him I needed more money, why did the white man have to make a black man do what he should have been doing all along?"

"I don't know, but I hope he pays it. Just because they told him to don't mean he will. I have been trying to get mine for years."

"Well, we'll be right back in court. Let me go, girl, time to go feed these kids. I'll talk to you later."

"Ok, bye."

Things were looking better since Jacob was paying out more money, but the car was starting to give me trouble again and a lot of the money went to keeping it running.

"Sara, it is hard paying you all this money. You struggling and I'm struggling. I just got a place. Why don't ya'll come live with me and you don't have to pay no mo' bills?"

"Oh, no, Jacob, you done said a lot of things before that you didn't mean. That's why I'm in the mess I'm in today, listening to you. No matter how hard I try, I just can't get ahead."

"At least try it. If you don't like it, you can leave."

"I know that. I don't need yo' permission to leave. I'll think about it."

Well, this is a chance to get ahead, Sara, I said to myself as I thought about his proposal. *I know you don't like him, but use this as an opportunity to save up some money and get away from here. He done held you down all these year; this is yo' time to use him to get what you want.* I thought about it over and over again. I guess I'd do it. It could be my ticket out.

Chapter 18

I moved in with Jacob a few months later and I regretted it from day one. I knew right then and there I had to make my move. I really liked Brian a lot, but he was married and would never be mine. I had been messing around with him for two years and they were still married. There was nothing he could do for me. I was twenty eight years old and I was not going to take all those problems into the next decade of my life. I decided to call the recruiting office.

"Army recruiting office, Sergeant Warren."

"Hello, Sergeant Warren, my name is Sara Johnson and I'd like to know the age cut off for joining the army?"

"Thirty five," the voice on the other end said. "Are you interested?"

"Yes I am. I am twenty eight years old with two children and I would like to join. What do I need to do?"

"Well, first of all, you need to take a test to see where you stand, after that you take a physical. When you pass that, you'll be on your way."

Same stuff I heard eleven years ago. The only thing that changed was my family situation.

"When can I come take the test?"

"How about tomorrow?"

"That will be fine." I gave him my number, directions to my house, and told him I'd see him tomorrow.

I tossed and turned all night that night. I was so ready to get out of that situation and I didn't know what to do. The next afternoon, Sergeant Warren picked me up to go take the test. I took it and passed again with flying colors.

"Now that you've passed the test, are you ready to come join our team?"

"More than you'll ever know," I said proudly.

"There is one problem," the recruiter said reluctantly. "You have to give custody of your children to someone else while you're in training, or get married."

I knew it was too good to be true. I was not about to give my kids away to nobody. Man, I didn't want to marry Jacob's butt either.

That changed a long time ago. What in the world was I going to do? I guess I could always stay there and do what I was doing for the rest of my life. I didn't think so. I was getting the hell out of here.

"Ok. I'll get back with you," I told him.

♫♪♫♪♫♪♫♪

After much debate, I finally came to a conclusion. I had to get married. My first step was to get away, and then I would deal with Jacob later.

"Jacob, can I talk to you, please?" I asked, walking over to the couch where he was sitting.

"Yeah, Sara, what's up?"

"Jacob, you know my childhood dream was to go into the Army, right?

"Right."

"Well, the opportunity has presented itself again and I think this is my chance to do something good for the kids. Look at this place. I don't want to raise them here in the land of no opportunities. I want to raise them to have the opportunities I didn't. I want to let them know that there is more out there than this. I spoke to the recruiter and he told me everything was set for me to leave. The only problem was I have to give up custody of the kids or get married. I don't want to give my babies away. I guess the question I'm trying to ask is, can we get married so we can get the hell out of here? If I don't do it now, I will never leave. It is the least you can do. You are the reason I'm still here. Will you please do this for me? Will you marry me?" Can you imagine that? Here I was asking that Bozo to do what he promised to do eleven years ago. If he said no, then Angela would have to keep the kids. Enough was enough. I was out of there one way or the other.

"Yeah, Sara. I'll do that for you. I did hold you back and if this will help you forgive me for all the things I did and all the lies I told, I'll marry you."

"Thank you," I said and gave him a hug. I called the recruiter, and told him of my intentions.

♫♪♫♪♫♪♫♪

Jacob and I got married two weeks later. Not out of love, but for convenience. I took my marriage license to the recruiter, picked my job, and was leaving the next month. If I could have left the next day, I probably would have. I had no intentions of staying with Jacob. I used him like he did me all those years. I planned on divorcing him as soon as I could. What I had to do now was to prepare Shanna and Jaylen for my disappearance. It was going to be tough on them, but I knew it would be better for them in the long run. I would see them at my basic training graduation, anyway. *Sara, you did it, girl,* I told myself. *You're finally taking control of your own life instead of letting someone else control it for you. It took some time, but it's finally here. Now, all I have to do is tell Brian.*

I went to work and told everybody that was my last week working. They were all sad to see me go, but they were happy for me, too. I had grown especially fond of an older white lady named Marie. She was a mother figure to me. I looked up to her.

"I hate to see you go, girl," she said as we walked with our hands around each other's waist. "I remember when you came here. You had little, if any, self esteem. You thought so little of yourself and could not take it when you were complimented on your looks. Well, let me tell you something. You may have come in here an ugly duckling, sweetie, but you're leaving here a beautiful swan. I'm going to miss you, girl."

I laid my head on her shoulder and let the tears flow. It was people like her that I was going to miss the most. She had also planned a surprise going away party for me, which we had on Friday, my last day of work, and I really was surprised. I was ready to go, but leaving that place was like leaving my family. I had one more thing to do before I left.

I asked Brian to meet me on the fishing bank where we used to go after work. He had no idea what I was about to say. "Brian, we have had some good times together, haven't we?" I said, holding his hand.

"Yes, we have."

"You have always treated me really, really well and have always come through for me and I appreciate it, but with our situation being the way it is, there is no way I can go on like this. It is not fair to you, me, and especially your wife. I know you will never be mine and we both knew it was going to come to an end one day. Well, that day is today. I'm sorry, but I can't see you anymore. You are a good man and I wish our situation was different, but unfortunately, we have to accept things as they are. I have some fresh new opportunities ahead of me and what I have to do now is go for it. I've waited an awfully long time for this to happen and I have to move on. Do you understand?"

"You go for it then, Sara. This is what you've always wanted. You are so special, I want you to be happy." I reached over and gave him a big hug. "I don't want to let you go," he said, still holding me with tears in his eyes. I let him hold me as long as he wanted because I knew that would be the last time he would hold me. "I am going to miss you," he said, finally releasing me.

"I am going to miss you, too." I took my fingers and wiped away his tear, kissed him on the cheek, and told him good-bye.

Chapter 19

"Get off that bus! Do you hear me? Hurry up! You better hurry up! Stop right there, private! You hear me talking to you? Drop and start pushing! You better start pushing! Bet you want your mama now, don't ya? Well, yo' mama ain't here and you gonna listen to me! I'm your mama now!" Boy, those drill sergeants had us running around like crazy. We didn't know if we were coming or going. Girls were crying and the ones who weren't crying were getting ready to. Not me, though. I was used to people yelling and insulting me, plus, I was older and had already been through some things. Most of them were just leaving home for the first time.

We did all kinds of training. We worked with guns I had never heard of, marched twelve miles with thirty five pound ruck sacks on our backs, and we had to keep our barracks so clean you could eat off the floor. We had to be up every morning by 0400 and lights were out every night at 2100. At the end of the day, we were so tired, we longed for our beds. It was hard mentally, but the gas chamber was cruel. We did get to use the phone every other day, and I talked to the kids as often as I could. I made a lot of friends because we always had to work as a team. The strong helped those who were weak. It was eight weeks of hell, but it was well worth it.

♫♪♫♪♫♪♫♪

I was so glad when graduation day came. I finally got a chance to see Shanna and Jaylen. Mama came along, too. "Hey, Mama! Hey, Mama!" they both screamed at the same time when they saw me. I ran to them and spun them around.

"You guys have gotten so big." It had only been two months, but kids grow fast.

"I missed you, Mama," Jaylen said.

"I missed you, too, baby," I said, giving him another big old hug.

"You been a good boy?"

"No," Shanna yelled.

"Yes I have," he said defensively.

"Uh uh, Mama. He peed in the bed."

"No I didn't, Shanna." He said glaring his eyes at her.

"That's ok if you peed in the bed, I know you still my big boy. Shanna, who did yo' hair?"

"Daddy," she said shamefully. She had plaits going all over the place.

"I did the best I could," he said.

"I know. Come here and give me a hug," I told him. I did kinda miss him. "Mama, I'm glad you came."

"Chile, I wouldn't have missed this for the world. You look sharp in that uniform. I am so proud of you."

"Thanks, Ma. It was hard, I ain't gonna lie, but I wanted to make you proud of me. It took me a while, but I didn't give up. Well, the good thing about it is that it's all behind me now."

"Come on, Thompson, we're about to start lining up," one of the soldiers said.

"Ok, ya'll, the ceremony is 'bout to start. I'll see you I a few minutes," I said, rushing off.

Standing on that parade field was one of the proudest moments of my life. I was finally living my dream, and that was something nobody could take away from me.

"Come on, ya'll, let's get out of here and do something," I said to my family, heading toward the parking lot after the ceremony was over. They only got to stay for a few hours and I wanted to spend every minute I could with them.

After I graduated basic, I went to my specialty school. I had to stay there another twelve weeks before going to airborne school. It was harder than basic training. They taught us how to fall. Could you believe that? Who did not know how to fall? We had to run four miles every single morning and there were no days off. I felt like I was training for the Olympics. On top of that, we had to run everywhere we went during the day. That was a lot of running. In order to graduate, we had to jump out of an airplane five times. That was challenging to me considering I was afraid of heights. We were up so high we couldn't see the ground, but when they put that chute on your back and told you to go, you better go or they would push you out of the plane. When I jumped out for the first time, I was so scared I thought I was going to have a heart attack. I was up so high, I didn't think I was ever going to touch the ground. It was much easier the second time though, but when we had to do a night jump, the fear returned. It was so dark I couldn't see my hand in front of my face, but I did it. I was glad when that school was over. I knew I was going to be stationed close to home without actually being there and I liked that, but most importantly, I liked the fact that I was finally a soldier girl.

♫♪♫♪♫♪♫♪

"You know Jacob was messing around while you were gone, don't you, Sara?" JaLisa told me soon after graduation. Here we go again with the same old shit. She had just killed my high.

"Who was it this time?" I asked reluctantly.

"Billy Jean."

"Billy Jean, the crack head?"

"That would be her."

"Lord have mercy! He done hit rock bottom. You mean to tell me that after all I just went through, I got to come back here to the same old shit? What a shame," I said, shaking my head.

JaLisa was good at keeping me informed on whatever was going on back home, but I just wasn't feeling it that day.

"So, it's Billy Jean now, huh Jacob?" I asked him later that night. I really didn't care, but I was so sick and tired of being disrespected.

"What you talking about, Sara?"

"Nothing, Jacob. Nothing at all," I said.

"Nothing happen between us, ok? What I want with a crack head?"

"A nut!" I said, looking him dead in his eyes.

"Girl, you crazy."

"I am? Ok!"

"What does that suppose to mean?"

"Like I said, Jacob, nothing at all. End of conversation," I said and left the room. That coward never owned up to anything.

When I got to my duty station at Ft Bragg the next week, my squad leader briefed me what I would be doing and also said we would be going to the field a lot. We would do physical training in the mornings and work call was at 0900. I didn't care. I was just glad to be in the Army. My only concern was what I going to do with Shanna and Jaylen when I went to the field. I would probably have to stay with Jacob a little longer than I had planned.

♫♪♫♪♫♪♫♪

"Jacob, I don't care how you take this, but I am pregnant again and if you don't want to stick around, see you later. I ain't going through what I went through with Jaylen," I told him after coming from the doctor a couple of years later.

"Hey, calm down," he said, coming over to me. "I ain't gonna trip. If it makes you happy, I'm ok with it."

"Well, I was just letting you know," I responded, puzzled. "You know you got a track record for running."

"Hey, not this time."

I knew how it happened, I just couldn't believe it. My life was already a train wreck and I just kept on getting pregnant. I couldn't understand why some women couldn't get pregnant, while others, all you had to do was say the word and bam. I still went to work every day and did what was expected of me.

I loved what I was doing. Of course, there were some bad days, but overall, I was glad I made the decision to join. I moved up the ranks pretty fast. It didn't take long for me to make Sergeant Thompson. I liked the sound of that. I was able to move the family, including Jeremy, my new bundle of joy, from an old trailer to a brick house near the base. It was a beautiful, big house in a nice area. It was a two story brick house with a one car garage, three bathrooms, a laundry room, a den, a living room, a formal dining room, plus an eat in kitchen and three bedrooms upstairs. It had a patio off the den. A few months later, I got my first brand new SUV, a Nissan Pathfinder. It was midnight blue and fully loaded. I loved the life I had. Of course, Jacob did, too. If anything, it should have made him feel guilty. Why couldn't he have done this for us? Now, he was reaping the benefits.

♫♪♫♪♪♫♪♫

Mama invited us to come to her house for a cook out one weekend. She had recently moved into a subsidized housing unit back home, so we knew we were going to see some familiar faces. One of my old girlfriends, Teresa, had come by to see me while I was there. I hadn't seen her in a couple of years and just like JaLisa, she knew everything that went on in town. Teresa was your typical girl; nice looking with light brown hair that she kept in braids, and light brown eyes. She was nicely built, but she had one downfall. Her mouth. It ran like a refrigerator.

My brother, Terrance, was there cooking on the grill. Cooking was what he loved most. He owned his own restaurant and was doing so well, he was considering opening up another one. He stood six one and was two hundred pounds. A lot of people said he looked like Lawrence Fishburne. His wife, Brandi, was really the brains behind the operation. Everybody called her boss lady 'cause if it wasn't done her way, it wasn't getting done. They had one daughter, Kayla.

My brother, Marcus, was on his way over. He was a smaller version of Terrance. He worked for a small printing company and was a playa, or so he thought. That was why he never got married. Everybody was catching up on the latest gossip.

"You look good, Sara," Teresa said. "The military has been good to you. I am glad you didn't let Jacob keep you down."

"I'm doing ok. I often think about all those years I wasted working all those different jobs trying to make it. I ain't doing too bad now."

"You know he was going with Billy Jean while you was gone, don't you?" she said. How did she flip that on me?

"Teresa, me and Jacob talked about that and he said nothing happened."

"Well, she just told me to tell him that he had some good dick."

I dropped my plate. "No, she didn't?"

"Yes, she did," Teresa said, eating her fish like she hadn't said a thing.

Billy Jean lived right across the street from my mama. She had just come out her door when Teresa told me. Billy Jean was a crack head and was considered the town's trash, so you know how that made me feel. Rumor was, every man in town had fucked her. She didn't have no hair, her skin was dry and scaly, she was shaped like an egg, and she had a missing tooth in the front. She'd had her first child at fifteen and, so far, nobody had claimed it.

"I'm going over there and ask her. I had been asking Jacob about this for some time now and he has always denied it."

"You know they say that's his baby, too."

Teresa didn't know when to stop. She went straight for the jugular. Billy Jean did have a baby soon after I got back. My blood was boiling.

"Wait right there. Billy Jean!" I yelled, walking out of my mama's yard into the street.

"What?" she yelled back as she came to meet me looking all haggard.

"I got a question to ask you." I was so mad my head was pounding. We were standing nose to nose and people were starting to gather around. "You been sleeping with Jacob?"

"What did he tell you?"

"Don't worry about what he told me, I am asking you."

"Whatever he said." I wanted to knock another tooth out right then and there. "Naw, I ain't been sleeping with him, 'cause if I was, you wouldn't have him," she said nastily.

"Is that his baby?" I asked, knowing full well I wasn't gonna get a straight answer.

"Not as I knows of. Now what?" she asked like she was challenging me to a fight.

"This," I said and slammed my fist across her face. She stumbled back surprised, then rammed her head into my stomach, knocking me down to the ground. I hung on to her by her shirt and started beating her in the side of her head. I could hear the crowd egging us on. I wanted so much to bite her, but didn't want to get HIV.

"Let go of me, bitch!" she yelled, trying to pull herself away. We separated for a split second and she punched me in the mouth. I grabbed her by the foot as she went to stand up and pulled her back down. I took my fingernails and gouged them into the side of her neck.

"Get off her!" I heard a familiar voice yell and looked up to see Shanna kicking her in her side. She then grabbed her by her hair and tried to pull her off me. Once free from her grasp, I landed another blow to the side of her head. Jacob came running and grabbed Shanna, who had started fighting Billy Jean's oldest daughter. Terrance came and grabbed me, and Billy Jean's brother came and got her. It was so many people around, but I didn't see none of them until that moment. The only person I wanted to see was the one whose skin was under my fingernails. In the distance, I heard sirens.

"Get yo' own man, bitch. Don't you ever fuck with mine again, do you hear me?"

"Get the fuck out my face," she said as she tried to jump me again. The sirens were close now so the crowd started dispersing. I walked back to my mama's and sat on the porch.

"What the fuck you looking at?" I asked Jacob and jumped up to go jump on him, but Terrance grabbed me and told me to sit down. Ma brought me a towel to wipe the blood off my face and arm. "Let's go, yall," I told them. "Where is Shanna?" I asked, looking around nervously.

"She's over here with me," Mama said.

"You alright?" I asked her.

"Yeah, Ma, but she scratched me. I'ma git her."

"She ain't worth it, baby, and he ain't, neither," I said, looking over at Jacob who better not had said anything. "Thanks, Teresa. You just don't know how much you've helped me today. Jacob has no more power over me. I don't know what I'm going to do when it's time to go to the field, but God will make a way. Shanna, get Jaylen and Jeremy and let's go."

Jacob came to get in the truck. "Not you, you bastard. You stay up here with yo' bitch." Shanna locked Jeremy into his car seat, I hugged Mama and Terrance bye, got in the truck, and pulled out of her driveway. I rode right past the three police cars that were gathering information and yelled to Billy Jean, "You can have him," as I drove down the road.

Chapter 20

I don't know why I was so mad at Jacob, he had been running around on me for years. If I was mad at anybody, it should have been at myself for allowing it. I let him treat me in a very disrespectful way for years so it was just as much my fault as it was his, but I promised myself that I would not let anyone else mistreat me. I thought if I stayed with him things would get better, but nothing changed. I couldn't believe I got so angry that Shanna and Jaylen had to see me fight. I guess that was the last straw. I had always wanted the kids to grow up in a healthy environment, but all they ever saw was me struggle.

"Mama, are you ok?" Shanna asked me as I lay across my bed. Jaylen came in behind her.

"You guys come over here and sit down. I want to talk to you. I am so sorry for what happened today. I did not mean for that to happen and you will never see me behave that way again."

"It's not your fault, Mom. For years I have seen how Daddy treated you. How come you blame yourself?"

"Because I allowed it, Shanna. I wasn't strong enough to do anything about it. Shanna, please don't ever let anyone treat you that way and, Jaylen, you are so young, you probably don't understand, but don't you mistreat women. I have tried to raise ya'll the best I knew how. I never felt like anybody ever loved me. In fact, nobody has ever told me that, including your daddy. I think that is why I allowed him to do those things to me. I never knew how it felt to be loved, but I love you guys, ok? Never doubt it. I will do all I can to help you grow into healthy adults. I may not have had the best upbringing myself, but I know how it feels to be abused and I will never do that to you guys. Shanna, you are tough girl. Where did you get that from?"

"I don't know, Mama, but I won't going to let nobody mess with you. If they mess with you, they got to mess with me."

"I didn't know what was going on. I went in the house and got some juice and when I came back, it was a big fight going on. I didn't know it was you, Mama," Jaylen said. "I would have threw a rock or something."

I wanted to laugh. "You will never see that again, ok?"

"Ok, Mama."

"Mama, what about Daddy, is he coming back?" Shanna asked.

"No, baby, I cannot allow him to continue to mistreat me. I have given him too many chances. I trusted him to give us a good life, but he could not provide one for us. I am not going to carry him. It is going to be hard, but we can make it, right?"

"You are the one who been taking care of us, anyway, so I know we are going to make it. You have done a good job, Mom. Be proud of yourself. I was watching you when you didn't know I was watching and I am glad you are my mama," Shanna said, coming over to give me a hug.

"I am too, Ma," Jaylen said.

I gave them both a big hug and kissed them. "Now, ya'll go to bed. Jaylen, don't wake up your brother."

"I won't."

"Good night, Mom. I love you," Shanna said with tears in her eyes.

"I love you, too." I got up and gave her another hug. We stood there and cried for a few minutes. "See you in the morning."

"Good night." I liked the sound of those words.

Right when everything got settled down, the phone rang. "Hello?"

"Sara, can I please come home? I didn't do nothing with Billy Jean. I don't know why people keep lying on me. I know I have messed up in the past, but I am not that way anymore. Please, don't throw our marriage away."

"Jacob, our marriage was over before we got married. I cannot live with you anymore. You have never spoken to me with respect. All you have ever done was put me down and you know what's sad? I believed I was all the things you said I was. Why do you think I wanted to get away so badly? I wanted to get away from that negative environment. All my life I was told I wasn't going to be anything. I tried to escape it years ago and prove to people that I was somebody, but I listened to you and trusted you to take me away from that lifestyle only to realize that you were no different from everybody else. I have wasted so many years depending on you when you never had any intentions of doing what was right. Now, it is too late. I know now that I am somebody no matter what you or anyone else says. It took me years to realize that because of people like you. People who don't want nothing and don't want nobody else to have anything, either. You have kept your foot on my throat for way too long, now it's my turn to live. I used to want to live it with you, but now I know I have to live it without you."

"Well, I need to come get my stuff."

"No problem. I will have your things packed and waiting for you."

"Sara, please."

"Goodbye, Jacob."

♫♪♫♪♫♪♫♪

Jacob did come to pick up his things and tried his best to convince me to let him stay. "Jacob, please go. I don't want you here. When I look at you, I see pain. Please leave."

"What did you tell the kids?"

"I told them that things didn't work out between us and that you were not coming back."

"Where is Jeremy?"

"At the sitter's."

"Can I at least stay here until he comes home? I haven't seen him in over a week and I miss him, along with Jaylen and Shanna."

"They will be getting home from school soon. I have to run out to the store and do some shopping. You can come back later. I will make sure you see them. Now, will you please leave?"

"Yes, I'll leave, but I will be back."

I was cooking dinner when he came back by. He was in the room playing with Jeremy when I called them down to eat. "Shanna, get your brothers and ya'll come down and eat. Make sure you wash your hands, too."

"Yes, ma'am," she said. They all came down and sat at the table.

"Mama, is Daddy staying for dinner?" Jaylen asked.

"I don't think so, baby. He will come back another time, ok?"

"Ok," he said sadly. That was the main reason I stayed with him for so long. I didn't have a daddy so I wanted them to have one.

"I'll be back soon, ok, buddy?"

"Ok, Daddy, maybe we can go fishing."

"Yeah, we can go fishing."

"See you later, Daddy," Shanna said as he was about to walk out the door.

"Be good, girl."

"I will." They walked over and gave him a hug. He reached down and picked up Jeremy and gave him a hug.

"See you later, buddy."

"Bye," Jeremy said, not knowing what was really going on.

Chapter 21

Things were getting really busy at work. I was spending more time there than I was at home. We were preparing for a big inspection and things had to be perfect. I worked alongside of Sergeant Taylor, who had been there longer than me and knew exactly where everything was.

"I am getting ready to run out to the store to grab some drinks. Do you want me to bring you something back?" he asked after we realized we were going to be there for a couple more hours.

"No thanks. I am fine." I said, sounding exhausted from working so many long hours

"I will be back in a few."

"Hooah," I said as I continued to work. He came back with BK and brought enough back for me. "Thank you, but you didn't have to do that," I said.

"I know, but it's rude to eat in front of somebody when you are the only one eating."

"I got to cook when I get home, anyway."

"Is your daughter old enough to cook yet?"

"Yeah, but she cooks only when I am there watching her. She's not good enough to cook on her own yet."

"When are you going to invite me over for dinner?"

"I'm not."

"What? You're cold."

"I'm just keeping it real. I am going to take five and eat before my fries get cold."

"Not a problem. I think I'll join you." We ate and finished up for the night. We had to be at it again early in the morning.

♫♪♫♪♫♪♫♪♫

I had been by myself for months and it wasn't so bad. I actually liked the freedom. I was cleaning up when the doorbell rang. "Shanna, can you get that?" I yelled over the vacuum cleaner. "It's Sergeant Taylor, Mom. He wants to talk to you." I shut off the vacuum to see what he wanted.

"I brought over these files. I thought we could go over them."

"Sergeant Taylor, why didn't you call first?"

"I was in the area and thought I'd stop by."

"This is not a good time. I am in the middle of cleaning."

"It will only take a few minutes. This is the only time I will have this weekend. I am going out of town after I leave here."

"Ok," I said reluctantly. "Let's get it over with." We went into the den where there was plenty of room. We went over the material and were about to wrap things up when the doorbell rang again. "Excuse me. I'll be right back." I opened the door to find Jacob standing there.

"Hey, Sara, may I come in?"

"Jacob! You just can't just show up here anytime you get ready."

"I just want to see the kids," he said, pushing his way in. "Oh, I see you got company. Hey, I am Jacob, her husband," he said, walking into the den.

"How do you do?" Sergeant Taylor asked.

"I was fine until I walked in on ya'll's date."

"This is no date, Jacob, we're working," I said, pissed off.

"Oh, so that's your cover up?"

"Jacob, will you please leave?" I asked, very annoyed.

"No, I don't think so. You see, the last time I checked, my name was still on the mortgage."

"Oh, so you want to go there? Sergeant Taylor, can we finish this up another time?"

"Sure, just come in a little earlier on Monday."

"Not a problem, I'll be there. Have a good trip."

"See ya," he said as he walked out the door.

"What the hell is wrong with you, Jacob? We were working."

"Sure you were." He laughed.

"Look, we have been separated for months. Don't you come in here acting like you pay some bills around here because you don't."

"This is still my house, Sara."

"Oh yeah? Well, you used my money to get it."

"It doesn't matter, my name is still on the deed.

"Well then, you can have your house. We'll move and I am not paying another red cent. Let's see how long it takes before it goes into foreclosure. You can't even keep a job. You're still staying with your mother for Christ's sake."

He grabbed me by my throat. "Who do you think you are talking to, huh? Don't you ever talk to me that way again, do you hear me?" he said, throwing me onto the couch.

"I am calling the police. You messed up putting your hands on me," I said, getting up.

"You ain't calling nobody," he said, yanking the phone off the wall.

"Have you lost your mind?" I asked. "Get your crazy ass out of here."

"You going to pay, Sara, mark my word. You are going to pay."

"Pay for what? I already suffered my punishment when I was with you." He came over and slapped me so hard, my lip started bleeding.

"Hit her again," Shanna warned, holding my gun.

"Shanna!" I yelled, going over to grab the gun. "Give it to me."

"Get out!" she said, still pointing the gun at him.

"Shanna, I am your daddy. Put the gun down," he said, shocked.

"I'm telling you for the last time, get out of this house." He looked at me glaring his eyes.

"Daddy, as much as I love you, you will never put your hands on my mama again or I'll kill you."

"Shanna, that's enough," I said. Jacob looked at her and backed out the door. "Shanna, what is wrong with you, girl?" I said, taking the gun.

"Nothing, Mom. I have watched you get abused long enough. Enough is enough, besides, it wasn't no bullets in it anyway, but he don't know that. He'll think twice before he comes back in here acting crazy."

I ended up staying in the house. After Shanna played Jessie James, Jacob stayed away. He would call and talk to the kids and since Shanna had a license, she would take them to meet him at a designated place. I took them to see their grandparents every now and then, but I hadn't seen him since he threatened me. He had poisoned all his family against me, which was ok. They didn't do anything for us, anyway.

Chapter 22

I was able to attend college while in my unit and met a couple of girls, Cheryl and Tiffany, from my English class.

"Hey, girl, this class is hard. I don't know if I'm going to pass," Cheryl said to me one day in the snack bar. She was about my height, five-three, and probably wore a size twelve in pants. She had mocha colored skin and wore her hair in a bob.

"Yes, you will. I'll be your tutor, but when we get into math, that's a different story. You will have to be *my* tutor."

"Deal."

"Hi, I know you already know my name, I'm Tiffany, but everybody calls me Tiff." Tiff was the complete opposite. She had a very light complexion and stood about five-six. She weighed about one thirty-five and wore her hair in long braids.

"Hey, I'm Sara. Do ya'll have time to sit down?"

"Just for a minute. I got another class to go to," Tiff said.

"Me too. Are you in the military?" I asked Cheryl.

"No, my husband, Kenny, is."

"Oh, ok."

"What about you?"

"Yeah, I'm in."

"How long have you been in?" she asked again.

"Not long enough. I still have a ways to go."

"Kenny, too. He has been in for close to fifteen years."

"Do you live nearby?"

"Yeah. I live in College Park."

"I live close by there in Kendalwood. What about you, Tiff?" I asked. "You sitting over there so quiet."

"I am active duty, too, and right now I'm living on post with my son, Terrell. I am about to get out though and go to school full time."

"Where are you going back to?"

"Virginia."

"Oh, ok. I stayed in Virginia for a little while years ago. I liked it pretty good. Well, maybe we can hang out sometime. It will be good to have somebody to talk to other than my children for a change."

"Sounds good to me. Kenny goes to the field a lot. It gets boring when he's gone, so yes, we can do that."

"Ya'll can count me in. I like to have fun, too," Tiffany said. "How about next Saturday night? I don't know if you ladies like comedy, but there's a great comedy club in Raleigh called Charlie Goodnights. It also has a restaurant which can be a bit pricey, but the comedy act is usually off the chain," she continued.

"I've never been to a comedy show before, so I think that will be great. How much does it cost to get in?" I asked.

"I don't know. It's been a while since I went, but I can check it out and let you guys know."

"Sounds like a winner. What about you, Cheryl?"

"I'm sure it won't be a problem. Kenny has been trying to get me to get out of the house for months. I'm looking forward to it."

"Ok, girls. It looks like we getting ready to have ourselves some fun," Tiffany said.

"Well, I got to run, it's time for me to go to my next class. I'll see you guys tomorrow," I said.

"Alright, take care," they both said.

Shanna had grown up to be a beautiful young woman. She had long, slender legs and the shape of an hour glass. She was around one hundred and thirty pounds, she kept her hair cut close, and her caramel colored skin was cocoa butter smooth. Her eyes were dark and her brows had a natural arch to them. Her lashes were so thick, she didn't need to wear mascara.

"Shanna, you'll be graduating soon. How does it feel?" I asked, getting ready to go plant some flowers.

"It feels great. I talked to my ROTC instructor today and told him I was interested in the Reserves."

"Are you sure you want to do that? You know you will have to go to basic training."

"Yes, I know. If it's ok with you, I'd like to stay here for a while and go to the community college after I graduate. The Reserves will pay for some of my college and I can work to pay for the rest of it."

"You can stay here as long as you like. I have some money saved up, so for your first year of school, all I want is for you to concentrate on school. What made you decide to go into the Reserves?"

"Well, I like the life you have given us. It started out rough, but I like the way it turned out. I don't think we would be where we are now if it wasn't for your drive and determination. I think the Army saved our lives. I guess I can show a little gratitude by giving them some of my time. That's the least I can do, but I hope I have that same drive and determination you got."

"You do. I have already seen it. You have to work on your temper, though. I don't want you out there getting into trouble."

"You don't have to worry about that. I like my freedom."

"Good, now come out here and help me pull these weeds.

"Mom, I have wanted to ask you this question for a while. When are you going to start dating again?"

"Girl, please. Dating is the last thing on my mind. I got two more kids to raise after you graduate. That's my main concern."

"That don't mean you have to raise them by yourself."

"I have always raised ya'll by myself, ain't I?"

"You know what I mean. Has the divorce become final yet?"

"Any day now."

"Is that what you're waiting on?"

"No, Shanna, that is not what I'm waiting on. I don't know. I tried dating a few months after me and your daddy separated, but that guy was a raving lunatic. I think he was bipolar. One minute we would be laughing and having fun and the next, he was the exorcist. Plus, he questioned me about every man I talked to. One time he told me he didn't want me talking to nobody but him. That's when I had to say bye-bye. I had already been through enough with Jacob, and I didn't want another busta, so after that, I decided to just be by myself. It's not bad, in fact, I enjoy it."

"But, don't you get lonely sometimes?"

"Sure, but all I have to do is remember him and your daddy, and I am not so lonely anymore. Listen, if I have to be in a drama filled relationship, I'd rather be by myself. Is that so bad?"

"I guess not, but Daddy has been going with somebody ever since ya'll separated."

"Your point? More power to him. I ain't surprised, but if he treats her like he treated me, I feel sorry for her."

"Well, I got a boyfriend."

"Oh really, since when?"

"We have been talking for a couple of months. He goes to my school."

"Unh, what's his name?"

"Morgan. He is so cute!"

"Baby, don't fall for him just because he's cute. You're setting yourself up for heartbreak. Looks ain't everything. He can look like Godzilla's brother as long as he treats you right. Girl, listen to me. If you have plans for your life, don't deviate from them, ok?"

"I won't. Don't worry, I am not having sex."

"Good. Am I going to get a chance to meet this fella?"

"Maybe. I got to make sure I really like him before I bring him home."

"Remember what I told you. Don't let nobody mistreat you."

"Oh, you don't have to worry about that. I'll be the last person he mistreats."

"Shanna?"

"I'm just kidding."

♫♪♫♪♫♪♫♫♪

When Saturday night came, I was really looking forward to having a good time. I hadn't been out in ages and didn't know if I was going to enjoy myself or not. "How do I look?" I asked Shanna and Jaylen as I spun around in the living room.

"You look great. Are you sure you're going out with the girls?" Shanna asked.

"Why, do I look sleazy?"

"No, you look sexy. That dress is hugging you, showing off all your curves."

"Ok, well I'm going to change."

"No, don't change. You are going to get plenty of attention in that."

"Yes, Mom, go change," Jaylen said.

"Why, Jaylen?" Shanna asked.

"'Cause, I don't won't those men drooling all over my mama."

"Ain't nobody going to be drooling over me, but I do think I'll go change into something else."

"I'll come help you find something," Shanna said. We finally decided on a pair of pencil-thin Baby Phat dark denim jeans with a white, tight fitting knit shirt and a half length matching jean jacket with sexy, strappy, black BCBG leather pumps. I accessorized in silver earrings and silver bangles. My hair was pinned up on top and my make-up was flawless. I had to admit, I did like what I saw when I looked in the mirror.

"Much better," Jaylen said, walking over throwing his arm around my shoulder. "Now you look like a lady."

"She looked like a lady before, just a sexy one. Have a good time, Mom," Shanna said as I was about to walk out the door.

"Ma, do you need me to come be your body guard?"

"No, Jaylen, I think I can handle myself. If not, you'll be the first one I call."

"Ok, one more thing."

"And, what might that be?" I asked turning around.

"Be home by twelve." Me and Shanna picked up the pillows on the couch and started beating him with them.

"You are too much, Jaylen." We laughed.

"Have fun," he said, giving me a hug.

We agreed to meet at Cheryl's house and ride together since Raleigh was about an hour's drive away. "Girl, we didn't think you were coming," Tiff said.

"I had a problem deciding on what to wear."

"That outfit is slamming. We better get going if we want to get there before it gets too crowded," she said. We got into her BMW X5 and headed down the road.

"It looks like we got here at a good time, there are still some parking places left," Cheryl said.

"I know. I just hope we can find a good table," Tiff said. We only had to stand in line a few minutes and once inside, we let Tiffany lead the way since she was familiar with the layout. She led us to a table just past the bar. "Is this good?" she asked.

"This is fine," Cheryl said. "We got a good view of the stage." The waitress came over to take our drink order.

"Give me a margarita on the rocks, please. What about ya'll?" I asked Cheryl and Tiffany.

"That sounds good to me. What you having, Cheryl?" Tiffany asked.

"Give me a Pina Colada."

"Ok, I'll be right back with your drinks," the waitress said and walked away.

"This is a nice club," I said, looking around.

"I know. I don't like going to those little hip-hop clubs. The kids in there are too young and don't know how to act. The last time I went to one, they had to close the place down early because of a fight. This place has a nice atmosphere and the men in here are not bad, either. Check out that one over there in the grey jacket. Don't he look good?" Tiffany said.

I looked over at him and said, "He looks alright."

"Girl, what is wrong with you? That Negro is fine."

"He looks good, I'll give him that, but aren't you dating somebody?"

"Yes, Derrick, and I love him very much, but that does not mean I'm blind. If a man looks good, he looks good and that's all it is to it. How long have you been separated?"

"Divorced now, I just got my papers in the mail."

"Oh, I'm sorry."

"For what? I'm not. I'm glad that part of my life is over."

"So, it looks like we have something to celebrate," Cheryl said as the waitress brought over our drinks. "To the future," she said as we held up our glasses to toast.

"To the future!" Tiff and I said as we clicked our glassed together.

"Hey, that's my song!" Tiff said when the Ying Yang Twins came on. "Come on, ya'll, let's dance." We went out on the dance floor and danced through three songs. When we finally got back to our table, it was time for the comedy act. When I sat down, a note was placed in front of my seat. I opened it up and it read: *Hi, my name is Darryl. I am sitting at the end of the bar in the blue jacket. If you don't mind, I'd like to buy you a drink.*

"What does it say?" Cheryl asked as I laid the note down on the table.

"Here, read it for yourself," I said as I turned around and mouthed, "No thank you," to him.

She read it and looked in the direction of the bar. "Are you going to let him buy you a drink?"

"No. A drink usually leads to a conversation, and I just want to have fun with you guys, and besides, if he wants to talk to me he can come over here."

"Girl, you are hard on a brother. Your ex must have done a number on you," Tiff said, puzzled.

"I am just not ready to get involved. Is that a crime?"

"I don't think so," Cheryl said. "When the right man comes along, you'll know it. Ok, ya'll, here comes the comedy act."

When a young, thin, tall black brother came out on stage with a neon green silk shirt on, purple pants, and dreadlocks, the crowd immediately started rolling. He had us laughing so hard our stomachs ached. His act lasted at least an hour, and he kept us laughing the whole time.

"That fool was crazy, wasn't he?" Cheryl asked, still laughing when the lights came back on.

"This was so much fun. I am so glad I wasn't sitting on the front row," I said, still laughing myself.

"You and me both. Do ya'll want to get something to eat before we leave?" Tiff asked.

"Yeah, let's get a basket of chicken wings," Cheryl said.

"Alright. Miss, can we get a basket of chicken wings and can you put some ranch dressing on the side?" Tiff asked.

"Sure, I will be right back with your order."

While we were waiting for our order, Darryl came over and introduced himself. "Hi, my name is Darryl, and I just wanted to stop by and tell you that you are looking lovely tonight."

"Hi, I'm Sara, and thank you."

"The offer still stands for that drink if you change your mind."

"Thank you, you are too kind, but I have already had my limit for tonight."

"Ok, maybe I'll talk to you a little later?"

"Maybe," I said, looking at the wedding band he was wearing on his finger.

"See ya in a little bit," he said, walking away.

"You go, Sara, he really wants to talk to you," Tiff said.

"Yeah, but I don't think his wife would like it too much. He was wearing a wedding band. I've had my share of married men. He can't do nothing for me. "

"Some men have a lot of nerve, don't they? If he wanted some play, he could have at least taken his ring off," Cheryl said.

"Here you go, ladies!" the waitress said, bringing our chicken wings.

"Um, these are good!" I said, dipping one into the ranch dressing.

"They got some pretty good food here," Tiff said.

"We got to do this again, ya'll," Cheryl said, eating the last wing.

"Since you're the one married, you let us know when," Tiff said.

"Ok, I will, but we should be able to do this at least once a month."

"Ok, ladies, are we ready to go?" Tiff asked, finishing off the last piece of chicken.

"Yeah, I'm ready, let's go." We got up to leave and on the way out, we saw Darryl sitting at a table kissing on another woman. When he looked up at me, I winked and waved bye.

♫♪♫♪♫♪♫♪♫

"Hey, Mom, did you have a good time?" Jaylen asked, walking into the kitchen where I was making breakfast the next morning.

"Yes, I did. Did I stay out too late?" I asked him jokingly.

"To tell you the truth, I don't even know what time you came in. I was knocked out shortly after you left."

"Good morning, Miss Thang," Shanna said, opening the door to the refrigerator to get out the juice. "How many men hit on you last night?"

"None."

"What? I don't believe that."

"I had a guy ask to buy me a drink, that's it. They were looking, but I acted like a lady."

"Mom, you got to loosen up, let your hair down, and have some fun."

"I did have fun and we are going to go out again soon. Call Jeremy down so we can eat."

The girls and I hung out one Saturday a month and always had a good time. We called it 'girl's night out.' I could not believe we had so much in common. I told them all about me and the things I had gone through and they understood why I was taking my time, but said they were stopping at nothing to finding me a man. Good luck to them because it was going to be hard. My past experiences made it hard for me to trust any man. I knew there were some good ones out there, I just didn't know if I was lucky enough to get one. I did help Cheryl throughout the semester and she came out of that class with a B+.

Chapter 23

"Ok, Shanna, this is your big day. How does it feel?" I asked walking into her room.

"Man, it feels so good. I can't believe it's finally here. Thank you so much for your support over the years and for letting me stay here to go to college. I think I'm going to join the Reserves before I start school, though, and get basic training out of the way. What do you think?"

"I think you should go to college and take ROTC like you did in high school and then join the Reserves as an officer. You are a very smart girl, and you'd make a great commander."

"Do you think so?"

"I know so. Am I going to meet Morgan today?"

"No, we broke up. We had different plans. We're still good friends, though."

"Congratulations, sis," Jaylen said, walking into her room. "I can't wait 'til I graduate."

"Thanks, bro," she said.

"Oh, and why is that?" I asked Jaylen, slightly offended.

"No offense, Mom, it's just one of those things that you look forward to in life. I want to join the military, too."

"Don't rush life, son. Before you know it, you'll be stretched so thin, you'll long to be back in high school. Your time will come sooner than you think. Life goes by rather quickly."

"I know. It's just exciting seeing my big sis going into her next phase of life."

"I ain't going nowhere yet, I'll still be here getting on your nerves."

"Ok, guys, we better get going. I don't want you to miss your own graduation."

I could not believe how fast time went by. It seemed like yesterday I was holding Shanna in my arms and, today, she was graduating high school. I was glad Jacob and his mother was able to attend. He and Shanna had a strained relationship after she pulled the gun out on him, but he knew he was wrong for his behavior that day and had not behaved like that since. I had never tried to turn the kids against him because, after all, he was their daddy. Just because things didn't work out between us didn't change that fact. They were old enough to form their own opinions about him. I didn't have to say a word.

He sat two rows ahead of me, but kept looking back. I knew he really wanted to say something, but didn't have the nerve to. I was doing well in my life and was looking quite good and, sometimes, I think he envied me because his life hadn't changed at all. I knew he wanted me back and when I saw how much he'd changed physically, I felt kinda sorry for him. He was still half working, drank all the time, had gained about thirty pounds, mostly in his belly, and he was starting to look really old for his age. But, that was his life now. I was no longer under his spell.

"Thank you for coming," Shanna said to her dad and grandma.

"You know I had to come and see by grandbaby walk across that stage," Lucy said, giving her a hug. "Yo' daddy told me you were going to go to college. I am glad to hear that. You stay as far away from the Army as you can."

"I am going to join the Army, Grandma. The Reserves."

"Well, at least you don't have no kids to abandon," she said, looking at me.

"Grandma, I love you and I am glad you came, but I will not stand here on the happiest day of my life and let you insult my mama when you know good and darn well her life would have been completely different if it wasn't for my daddy. She has always wanted to give us a better life and she did, no thanks to him. Now, if this is what you came to this graduation for, you can just leave."

"She done poisoned ya'll against us, ain't she?"

"Grandma, you guys are the ones with all the venom, she was just your prey. Thank you for coming, Daddy, but I think Grandma is ready to leave."

Lucy looked at me with the most evil look I think I had ever been given. "Jaylen, I'll give you a call later, ok? Jeremy, you be a good boy."

I could see the hurt in their eyes, but I tried to fix things like I always did. "Jaylen, you and Jeremy go over there with Shanna so I can take this picture." They took lots of pictures showing all their teeth with Shanna holding up her diploma. I was determined not to let the Thompsons spoil our day, and they didn't.

♫♪♫♪♫♪♫♪♫♪

I was glad Shanna stayed at home and went to college because she was a big help around the house. She was able to cook on the days I had to work late and with some of the money I'd been saving, I was able to help her buy a car. It wasn't a new one, believe me, just something to get her back and forth to school. Of course, I asked Jacob for help, but we all knew the answer to that question. Jaylen got his license and I told him I'd help him once he got a job and started saving money, but he didn't want me to do that for him. He said he was a man and would get a car when he could afford it. I had already done enough and he didn't want any handouts; that was what was wrong with his dad.

Since he walked to school, he was able to participate in sports and not worry about not having a way home. He loved running track and was good at it. The team almost made it to the Regionals, but lost by a few points. His proudest moment was when his picture made the town paper. Jaylen stood five-eleven and weighed about one hundred and seventy pounds. He had a slightly darker complexion than Shanna but he still had light skin. He had a thin mustache and had those same dark eyes and wavy hair. I said wavy, not good, and when people saw him and Shanna together, they knew they were sister and brother. They got most of their features from Jacob. Jaylen had a muscular build from working out and running track, and was popular with the girls, although he said he didn't have time for them.

Chapter 24

Shanna was completing her second year of school when we experienced one of the most horrifying days in our history. One day out of the blue, all Hell broke loose. Two planes flew into the World Trade Center and one into the Pentagon. We were put on high alert and there was chaos everywhere. That day changed our lives forever.

"Ok, troops, I want you to go home and make sure your bags are packed. I just want you to know that you may be called out at any time, so make sure you are close to your phones. We are trained to be out of here within eighteen hours and from this point on, we are on standby. That means no drinking until further notice. Soldiers, we are at war," the First Sergeant told us.

We started training vigorously, and before I knew it, I was on a plane going into combat. I couldn't believe it. I wasn't afraid. I was doing what I was trained to do, but I just didn't think I would actually be going to war. I was prepared and knew that what I, and so many others, was doing was going to make a difference in America's freedom. I was proud that I was able to do my part, and as long as my kids were fine, I was fine. If this was my destiny, then so be it. They knew that I loved them. I just thanked God Angela was able to keep the boys while I was away. I couldn't leave them with Mama because of her drinking and Jacob didn't even have a place to stay himself. Shanna remained at home so she could finish school and attend her weekend drills. I prayed she didn't have to come over here; one in the family was enough.

"You doing ok, Sergeant Thompson?" the Lieutenant Commander asked me.

"Doing fine, Sir."

"Good. We won't be over there long. We are going to go get him and go back home."

"Hooah, Sir," I replied.

We arrived in Afghanistan late that night so I really couldn't see much of anything. We had to attend several briefings before we were shown to our hooches. I was escorted to a big, tan colored tent that had several cots in it. It smelled damp and dusty, but I didn't complain because I knew that was going to be my home for the next six months. When we got up the next morning for formation, I was able to see my surroundings for the first time, and man, there were tents everywhere. We had no inside plumbing except for the shower point, which was two blocks away. It wasn't too cold considering I went during the winter, but it wasn't hot, either. I did what I had to do and counted the days 'til I could return back home. Experiencing conditions such as those made me appreciate being an American citizen.

There were many long, hard days in that desert, but after seven and a half months, it was finally time to return home, but unfortunately, we still hadn't got him. There were two wars going on by that time, so soldiers were deploying left and right. Shanna's unit was activated and she had to go, too. I hated it so much for her and wished I could have traded places with her. She was going in as a commissioned officer, which wasn't bad, but she was still in harm's way. She said she wanted to pay her dues, she was definitely going to pay them now. I was proud of her, though, she was tough as nails and deep down inside, I knew she was going to be ok.

♫♪♫♪♫♪♫♪

I had been back several months and was in training for a second deployment when I came down on orders to go to another post, Aberdeen Proving Ground, Maryland. It was just me and the boys since Shanna still had a couple of months left of her deployment. I sure did miss her. We had been together all my adult life. The war separated a lot of families, but she knew she could come stay with me anytime she wanted. I put the house up for sale and we headed to Maryland. I didn't know anybody there, but we were on our way. Believe it or not, Jacob wanted to come, too. I didn't know what he was thinking, if he was thinking at all.

I met a lot of friends at Bragg and I could still hear Cheryl saying, "Girl, I am so sorry to see you go. We have been friends for some years now and I have really enjoyed our friendship. Just because we got some miles in between us don't mean we still can't be friends. I hope you come back this way again. Oh, and by the way, I'm still looking for you a man. Remember, keep looking forward."

Looking forward was the only way I could look, but looking back wasn't so bad, either. It reminded me of where God brought me from.

Chapter 25

Maryland was a Mid-Atlantic state and depending on where you lived, the weather could be hot and humid in the summer and cold and snowy in the winter. Aberdeen was borderline. I had never worked with civilians before, so I didn't know if it was something I was looking forward to or not. I got there and got settled in pretty quickly. I moved on base because I wasn't familiar with the area. It was different from what I was used to, but I liked it and so did the boys.

We moved during Jaylen's last year of school and I had to make sure the school system was the same as the last. I didn't want him being held back because of the grading differences. He had no problem and soon joined the track team. Jeremy never had a problem meeting new friends. He had such a good spirit; kids were naturally drawn to him. My new job required me to do a lot of traveling, but because of the budget, I wasn't able to go too often. It wasn't a bad transition from soldier to civilian, but I did miss the soldiers.

I was there about six months when a tasking came down and someone needed to go to Kuwait. Since I was one of the highest ranking soldiers there, I was pretty much volunteered. I was disappointed since I had just gotten there, but since the tasking wasn't for too long and the boys said they'd be ok, I prepared for my next deployment. Angela agreed to keep them again. I didn't think I would have made it without her.

"How long are you going to be gone this time, Mom?" Jeremy asked when I walked into his room.

"Only for a few months. I will be back before you know it."

"Are you sure you are going to be ok? I don't want anything to happen to you."

"I don't either, son, but I will be ok. I will be going to Kuwait, it's not as dangerous as Afghanistan."

"It's dangerous everywhere if you ask me."

"Maybe all of this will be over soon and nobody will have to leave again. How about that?"

"That will be great, but do you know what?"

"What?"

"One day, I'm going to be doing the same thing."

"Oh really?"

"Yep. If you and Shanna can do it, so can I."

"The military is not for everybody, son. You might want to think about it. You can go to college and be a doctor or teacher. That would be nice."

"Yeah, but I want to be a pilot."

"Wow, that sounds good. I wish you were flying the planes some of those times I had to jump out of them. I swear I thought those pilots were drunk most of the time the way they had us all sick."

"You wouldn't have been sick with me, it would have been a smooth ride," he said, smiling.

"Man, I'm glad you were here for my graduation," Jaylen said, standing in the doorway.

"Son, I would have took a court martial if I had to miss your high school graduation. I am just thankful that you are willing to wait 'til I come back to join the Navy. You didn't have to do that, you know?"

"I know, but it would have been hard on Jeremy if we were *all* gone. I will take good care of him and when you come back, it will be my turn."

"Thanks, Jaylen. I just hope you don't have to deploy when you do leave. It's hard enough when Shanna is gone. I don't know if I could take it if something happened to any of you."

"How do you think we feel? It is hard seeing our mother going to war. You are my most prized possession, so go over there and get back here, ok?"

"I'll do my best. Are ya'll ready to go?"

"Yeah, I guess," Jeremy said sadly.

"Ok, let's get your suitcases and head for the car. Angela is waiting for us," I said teary eyed. I hated leaving them.

Lord, please let this be the last time.

♫♪♫♪♫♪♫♫♪

"Hey, we're here!" I yelled as I entered Angela's house.

"Come on in," she said, coming into the living room. She was doing well for herself. She worked as a registered nurse at a local hospital and lived in a big two story, four bedroom, ranch style house. We gave our usual hugs and told the boys where to put their bags.

"Are you going to be ok?" she asked.

"I'll be fine, just take care of my babies."

"Girl, those brats are going to be fine. Don't be over there worrying about them. You know I'm going to take good care of them."

"I know, but I feel so bad leaving them."

"I know, but you shouldn't. Because of what you do, you have given them a great life. Now all you have to do is give yourself one."

"Angela, please don't start. I have a great life."

"You do to a certain degree, but you won't let yourself get close to a man. It's not natural, Sara. You need love, too."

"I got the love of my children and that's all that matters."

"If you say so, but they can only do so much."

"Maybe one day, Angela, maybe one day. Where is everybody?"

"Cheyenne is at the mall and I don't know where Vanessa is."

"What did you cook for dinner? I'm starved."

"Go to the table and sit down. I'll fix you a plate. Do you think the boys are hungry, too?"

"No, I stopped at McDonald's and got them something." She cooked my favorite meal; ham, potato salad, and green beans, and it was delicious as always.

I had to leave the next morning. It was hard saying good-bye, but I knew everything was going to be alright. *Who is that calling so early?* I wondered when I heard the phone ringing. "Hello?"

"Hey, I'm glad I caught you before you left. How are you doing?" Shanna asked.

"I'm hanging in there, girl. How are you?"

"Ok. I was hoping I'd get to see you before you left, but my crazy schedule wouldn't permit it."

"That's ok, it's good hearing your voice. You won't be deploying again anytime soon, will you?"

"I don't think so, but my last deployment wasn't so bad. How are Jaylen and Jeremy?"

"They're doing fine. You know your Aunt Angela is going to spoil them rotten."

"I know. Did Dad call before you left?"

"Nope. I haven't heard from him in a while."

"What a shame. His loss though. He had a good woman and didn't know how to treat her."

"Shanna, I am so past your daddy."

"No, you're not, because if you were you would have moved on by now. You are letting him and the way he treated you hinder you from meeting someone who will probably be really good to you, but you won't give them a chance because of who? Daddy O."

"I'll meet somebody someday, and when I do, you'll be the first person I call."

"Ok. Mom, seriously, be careful over there. We'll be waiting for you when you get back."

"I will. I'll call the first chance I get."

"I love you."

"I love you more. I'll talk to you soon. Bye now."

"Bye." I hung up the phone, called Mama and told her bye, and that I'd see her in a few months.

♫♪♫♪♫♪♫♫

It took us two days to get there. We made a short stop in Germany before continuing on to Kuwait. When we finally arrived, the temperature was one hundred fifteen degrees and I was really surprised by our accommodations. Because of the special assignment I was on, I was able to stay in a building with AC and inside plumbing and showers instead of the two-man trailers with no inside plumbing. I had my own room, an Isuzu Trooper to drive, and a cell phone. That was pretty darn good to be on a deployment. It was much better than my last one.

Once we settled in, Sergeant Smith, the soldier I was replacing, gave me a brief overview of my new job. "You are going to like being here. What we do makes a big difference on what the war fighters eat, how they sleep, and, most importantly, how we provide protection for them when they are outside the wire. We are a valuable asset when it comes to their welfare and saving their lives. Are you ready for me to show you around?"

"I sure am," I answered, anxious to get started. We got into the truck and started on our way. As I rode around, I couldn't help but notice how much desert there was. It was sand as far as the eye could see.

"We get a lot of sand storms here and when we do, everything shuts down. No flights come in or go out during those times and sometimes they can last for days."

"Oh yeah? I wonder if I'll see one while I'm here."

"You will. Trust me, you will."

Our first stop was the motor pool, then to our company headquarters, and finally to the airfield terminal. That was where all our flights would be made. "We are going to stop in here and I am going to introduce you to Mike. He is a very valuable man when it comes to scheduling your flights. He has worked wonders for this team. He can get you flights that nobody else can get. I don't know how he does it, but he's just a genius when it comes to getting us in and out. If you ever need anything, he is the man to come to. He is a civilian contractor who used to be in the military and just retired a couple years ago. He's a good man, you'll like him."

We walked into this building that reminded me of two double wide trailers put together. We went down the hallway and entered a room that was occupied by two people; a white man and a Hispanic. "Sergeant Thompson, this is Mike, Mike, this is Sergeant First Class Thompson," he said to the Hispanic man.

"Hey, how are you?" I said, extending my hand to a six-foot, about two hundred and thirty pound MANDINGO. He was the biggest Hispanic man I had ever seen. His hair was straight and neatly groomed, his eyes were soft and gentle, his skin was like that of a baby, and he had the softest hands I'd ever felt on a man. I was intrigued by him.

"I'm fine, thank you. Pleased to meet you, and I'm glad to have you as a part of the team. Can I get you guys some water? I know it's hot out there," he said, speaking perfect English. If I had been talking to him on the phone instead of standing here in front of him, I would have mistaken him for white. He had no Spanish accent at all. He was simply charming.

"Yes, please," I said, feeling a bit parched.

"What about you, Smitty?"

"No thanks, I got some in the car."

"Well, Sergeant Thompson, what do you think of the place so far?"

"I think this is going to be interesting. This will be something I've never done before and I'm looking forward to doing my part."

"Well, good, I'm looking forward to working with you. If you need anything or have any questions, here's my card, give me a call. I have been around a couple of days so I know a few people."

"Thanks, I'll do that," I said, taking his card and putting it in my pocket. "Well, Sergeant Smith, are you ready to go?" I asked.

"Yeah, it's getting close to chow. We better go pick up everybody else and go eat. You take care of her, Mike."

"I will, you don't have to worry about that. When are you out of here?"

"In a couple of days."

"Well, if I don't see you anymore, take care, dude. It was a pleasure working with you. Keep in touch!"

"I will." They gave each other a half hug and we left to go get something to eat.

Chapter 26

Several days after Sergeant Smith and his team left, Sergeant Major Reynolds, my team leader, needed a flight to Balad, Iraq to track some equipment. "Sergeant Thompson, can you get me a flight out Thursday returning on Sunday?"

"Not a problem, Sergeant Major. I will go by the terminal as soon as I get finished typing this paper." I was actually looking forward to going to the terminal. It gave me the chance to see the Mandingo. "Hey, Mike. How are you today?"

"Hey, girl. I am doing fine, trying to stay cool. What can I do for you?"

"Sergeant Major needs a flight to Balad leaving Thursday returning Sunday. Do you think you can hook us up?"

"Yeah, I think so. Is he going to need accommodations?"

"I'm sure he will since he will be staying overnight."

"Ok, let me see what I can do. I will give you a holler later on today, alright?"

"Ok."

"Are they treating you alright up there?"

"Yeah, everything is going smoothly. I got pretty good team members."

"Good. Ok, I'll call you as soon as I hear something."

I left his office and went back to work. A couple of hours later the phone rang. "Task Force Tiger, Sergeant First Class Thompson speaking, may I help you, sir or ma'am?"

"Hey, this is Mike. I am calling to let you know that everything is a go with the flight to Balad."

"Great."

"He needs to be at the helipad at 1800."

"Thanks, Mike. You're the greatest."

"You're welcome. Hey, what you got going on tomorrow morning?"

"I don't know yet. Why?"

"Well, if you're not busy, do you want to have coffee?"

"Where can we get coffee at over here?"

"Green Beans. It's right next to the Post Exchange. If you have a few minutes, I'd love to take you there."

"Green Beans? What kind of name is that?"

"Strange, huh? But, they serve some great coffee."

"Give me a call in the morning and I'll let you know if I'm available. Things can get hectic around here sometimes."

"I bet. I'll give you a holler in the morning. Have a good night, girl."

"Ok, you too. See you tomorrow." *Um, I sure hope I'm not too busy.*

♫♪♫♪♫♪♫♪♫

"Hello?"

"Good morning, Mike."

"Hey, girl."

"Do you still want to go to Green Beans? I don't have anything going on this morning. This evening is a different story. I need to get out of the office for a while anyway."

"I know what you mean. Yeah, I still want to go. Can I come pick you up right now?"

"Yep. I'll be outside waiting for you."

"Ok. I'll see you in a few."

He picked me up and we rode around the block to the coffee shop. It was a really small building and there was a line waiting to order.

"You sure you want to stay?" I asked. "The line is pretty long."

"Yeah, the line goes pretty fast. See they just opened up another line," he said pointing to the counter. "Ok, we're next, what would you like?" he asked when we got close enough to order.

"I don't know. I normally drink regular coffee. What do you suggest?"

"Give me two Spiced Vanilla Chai Lattes with cinnamon," he said to the man behind the counter. "I think you'll like this. It is one of my favorites."

We picked up our coffee and found a corner table to sit down at. He pulled my chair out for me as I was about to sit down. A true gentleman.

"Umm, this is good," I said as I took a sip of my coffee. "What is the name of it again?"

"Spiced Vanilla Chai Latte with cinnamon."

"It's delicious."

"I thought you'd like it. So, tell me a little about Sergeant Thompson. What's your first name?"

"Sara."

"Can I call you Sara?"

"Sure."

"Ok, Sara, tell me a little about you," he said, getting comfortable in his chair.

"Well, I was raised in NC, I have three wonderful kids, I have been in the Army for fifteen years, and am currently stationed in Maryland."

"Maryland? What post in Maryland?"

"Aberdeen Proving Ground."

"Yeah, that's right. Do you like it there?"

"Yeah. I haven't been there long, but I heard it can have some brutal winters."

"Well, you won't be cold for a while because it gets pretty hot here."

"Who you telling? It didn't take me long to figure that out. What about you?" I asked.

"Well, I grew up in Colorado, talk about cold, but it is so beautiful. I joined the army right after high school and retired a few years back, but I couldn't get away from the troops. I love helping them. Here they are putting themselves in harm's way, the least I could do is to help make their job as safe as possible. I have been here a little over fourteen months and I like it pretty good. "

"I really admire the way you speak passionately about the soldiers. So many people don't understand."

"Oh, I understand. I used to be one. I know how tough it is."

"Are you married?"

"Divorced, but I got two great kids. They are my world."

"They should be. I love it when a man takes pride in his kids. You find so many who could care less."

"I know. It's a shame. I can't see how they do it, I love mine to death."

We talked on and on. It was something about that man. He made me feel so safe. I felt so good being in his presence. He listened so intensely when I talked. He didn't criticize or give an opinion, he just listened. I was really beginning to like him.

"Well, we need to be heading back. I don't want them to think I kidnapped you."

"Oh, they'll be fine. This was fun, we are going to have to do this again sometime."

"Believe me, we will," he assured me. We continued to talk as we walked to the car and right before I opened the door, he said, "Wait. I'll get that for you."

He opened my door and closed it behind me. *This man is definitely a keeper,* I said to myself.

When I got back to the office, there were plenty of things to catch up on. I had to track equipment, go out to units, and test new equipment that had just come in. Most of the work I had to do was computer related, so I turned the computer on to pull up the equipment log. *Let me check my email before I get started. I hope I got an email from the kids.* Oh, how I missed them. That was the hard part of this job, leaving the family. I knew the reason I was doing this was to give them a better life, but they definitely pulled on my heart strings. *Um, an email from Mike.*

Sara,

Thank you for coffee this morning. You are a wonderful person to be around. I love listening to you. I like it when you laugh. You have such a beautiful smile. You are so professional and carry yourself with so much class; I will always treat you with the utmost respect. You are a beautiful lady and I hope we can do this again sometime. Hope you have a good day.

Mike

Man, I didn't expect that. He definitely got my attention. Why couldn't he be in Maryland? I could see myself really loving him, but would he still love me after I gave him my heart? I didn't know if I was ready for that. My heart was telling me to go for it, but my mind was saying, *He will probably play you, Sara, remember Jacob? Don't do it to yourself again.* I was so confused, but at the same time, it felt so good.

We had many more coffee dates after that. We always had such a good time when we were together. He made me feel so good about myself. I felt a confidence with him that I never felt with any other man and not once had he tried to get me into bed, and there were plenty of opportunities. I had my own room and he had his own hooch. He really did respect me, but I just could not allow myself to get too close to him. There was no way I was going to give him the chance to break my heart. What I needed to do was focus on what I was there to do, but it was hard with the temptation I had in front of me.

♫♪♫♪♫♪♫♪

"Sara, remember I told you I was going on R&R soon?" Mike asked me a couple of weeks later.

"Uh huh, to Colorado, right?"

"Yeah, well, I'm trying to head out in the next couple of days. Do you want me to send you anything while I am gone?" I had heard that before. People saying they going to send stuff and you never got it.

"Ah, yes, if you don't mind."

"Make me a list and give me your address. I'll send it to you."

"Ok, thanks! I sure could use some stuff, you know they don't have a lot to choose from at the Post Exchange."

"I know, that's why I get all I can when I go home."

I gave him the list and told him, "Have fun. I'm going to miss our coffee dates while you're gone."

"Me too, but I'll be back before you know it."

A week after he left, I received the box from him. He sent it just like he said he would. He was truly a man of his word. That was a first for me. I really wanted that man. I wanted him bad, but I just couldn't. I did not want to get played again. He could be telling me anything. He might be home with his wife right now. But oh, how I missed him. *Baby, please, hurry back.*

Chapter 27

It was a long two weeks. I was in my office scheduling some appointments when the phone rang. "Task Force Tiger, Sergeant First Class Thompson speaking, may I help you, sir or ma'am?"

"Well, hello beautiful."

"Hey!" I said full of excitement. "When did you get back?"

"I got in late last night. Pretty tired, but I wanted to call and let you know that I made it back in. Do you have time for coffee?"

"I sure do."

"See you in a few." We drank our lattes and I listened as he told me what he did when he was home. "I brought you something back."

"You did?"

"Yeah, I forgot to bring it though. Why don't you come by tonight and watch a movie? I can give it to you then."

Here we go. I knew it was just a matter of time. "What movie are we going to watch?"

"I don't know, I got several. You can choose one."

"Ok. We quit work around 1900. Anytime after that is good. I'll call you."

"Um, sounds good. I'll see you tonight."

"Alright, see you later," I said as I was getting out of the car

I was really looking forward to 1900. It would be my first time going to his room. I hoped I could contain myself. The last thing I wanted was to have sex and then he started acting brand new. I had learned a lot over the years, respecting my body was one of them.

♫♪♫♪♫♪♫♪

"Hey, everybody," Mike said when he walked into the room later that night where we were all sitting.

"Hey, Mike. How's it going?" Sergeant Major asked him as he got up to shake his hand.

"Not too bad, can't complain," Mike said, returning his handshake.

"Thanks for everything you're doing for us. I don't think we would have gone to half of the places we went to if it wasn't for you and your connections. You have done a superb job."

"No problem, dude. That's what I get paid for. I am just glad I am able to help."

"You make sure you take care of Tommie tonight." That was the nickname they gave me.

"I am not a kid, Sergeant Major, I will be just fine," I said, feeling slightly embarrassed. Since I was the only female on the team, they were a bit overprotective.

"I know, I was just teasing."

"She is in good hands, Sergeant Major," Mike said.

"Don't wait up for me," I said and winked as I walked out the door. Once inside his room, I started looking through his movies to see which one we would watch. "Let's watch *The Skeleton Key*," I suggested, getting comfortable on the couch.

"Ok. Do you want something to drink?"

"No, thank you. I don't drink anything after 1900."

"Why is that?" he asked.

"I hate getting up in the middle of the night to use the bathroom."

"I heard that. At least you don't have to go outside like I do," he reminded me.

"I know. I had to do that when I was in Afghanistan, and I definitely don't miss it."

"Oh, let me give you the gift I brought back for you. When I was at the airport, I kept looking at this for some reason and I could not imagine why. On the way back, I was drawn to it again. Then, I realized why, you." He took out a round, blue Swarovski Crystal box. "Remember when you said you were an ugly duckling and one day you woke up and you were a beautiful swan?"

"Yeah?" I answered, puzzled.

He opened up the box and took out a crystal angel. He handed it to me and said, "Not only are you a beautiful swan, you are also an angel."

I was shocked. I was happy, but shocked. "This is so beautiful," I said, my eyes filling with water. "Thank you so much," I said, giving him a big hug.

As I pulled away, he looked me in my eyes and asked, "Can I have a kiss?"

"Of course you can."

I gave him the kiss I had wanted to give him for months and was completely speechless for a few seconds afterwards. I could not stop admiring the angel. *Me, an angel.* I loved the thought of it. It was the most precious thing anyone had ever given me.

"Do you like it?" he asked, knowing he had scored big.

"Like it? I love it!" I said and hugged him again. We didn't watch the movie, it watched us. We were so caught up in each other, who cared about a movie?

"Well, I guess it's time for me to go," I said, looking at my watch, not realizing how much time had passed.

"So soon?"

I wanted so much to stay and make love to him and I knew if I stayed any longer, I would have. "Yeah. You know how time flies when you're having a good time. I had a great time, but it's getting late."

"Ok, don't want to keep you out too late," he said, sounding disappointed. We got to my building and before I got out the car, he asked, "Can I have another kiss?"

I reached over and gave him an even juicier kiss than before. "See you later," I said as I got out of his car.

♪♪♫♪♫♪♫♪♫♪

I could not sleep that night. I tossed and turned. Mike was not your average guy. *He brought me a crystal angel,* I kept telling myself, *and he still didn't try anything.* Was he gay? Any normal guy would have tried to jump my bones. I had never met anyone like him in my whole life. I hated I would be leaving soon. I would definitely be glad to stay there with him, but my time was up in a couple of weeks. I knew when I left I would never see him again. I was falling in love with a man I knew I could not have.

When I got up the next morning, I checked my email like I always did first thing in the morning.

Sara,

I am truly glad that you liked the angel. You are a beautiful person and I love spending time with you. I am so glad you came on this deployment because I have had nothing but good times since you've been here. I know you are leaving in a couple of weeks and that's a bummer. I was hoping before you leave, we can spend some quality time together. I hope to talk to you soon.

Mike

"Quality time?" I *had* been spending quality time with him. I was with him all the time. As much as I wanted to, I couldn't go to bed with him and then leave in two weeks. I would not do that to myself and I would not do that to him.

Mike,

I had a good time too and I, too, hate that I am leaving so soon. Again, time flies when you're having fun. I know you want to spend quality time with me but I just cannot get intimately involved with you. I shared my painful past with you and right now, I am so afraid. You are the sweetest guy I have ever met and if there was anybody, it would be you, but this is not the time or the place. I really like your company and look forward to spending time with you, but if it's a physical relationship you're looking for, I'm sorry, I cannot do it. I hope you understand.

Sara

Those were the fastest two weeks in history. I did have coffee with Mike a couple more times and I was so glad I met him. I would never forget the impact he had made on my life. He was someone I knew I would be willing to give my heart to if the time was right. I felt so much compassion for that man and I hated I had to go, but I prayed this was not the end for us, just the beginning.

♫♪♫♪♫♪♫♪

"I am glad you were all able to attend this farewell party for Tommie. She has been an essential part of this team. She is the glue that mended us together..." Sergeant Major said at my farewell.

As I stood there, all I could think about was Mike standing there looking at me with sorrow in his eyes. I wanted to tell him so badly how I really felt about him, but what was the point? I was leaving, right? He knew I cared. I had already told him that, but I cared a lot more than I let on. I knew I was punishing myself and him for something someone else had done to me and I hoped and prayed things wouldn't always be that way. "So, Sergeant First Class Thompson, it was a pleasure working with you. You are one of the Army's finest. God speed!" Sergeant Major said in his closing statement.

"Speech, speech." I heard through all the applause. I really didn't know what to say.

"I really don't like making speeches, so I'm going to keep this short." I said when the clapping stopped. "You all have been wonderful to work with. I never thought coming on this deployment would make such an impact on my life. It will be an experience I'll never forget. I hope the friendships that were made here, just don't end here, but continue though out the rest of our lives." I said looking at Mike. "So let's keep in touch everybody. I'm going to miss you guys." I said finishing my speech. I mingled for a while then people started to leave. I knew this was the last time I would ever see Mike, so my eyes were locked on him as he made his way over to me.

"Well, I guess this is it." He said letting out a sigh.

"Yeah, it's that time. Thank you so much for everything Mike. I am so glad you were here." I said grabbing his hand.

"Same here. You got my email, write me sometime."

"I definitely will."

"Take care beautiful. It was a pleasure." He said kissing my hand.

"I will. You do the same, and the pleasure was all mine." I looked in his eyes and saw his soul, and it made a lump come in my throat. I had just let the love of my life slip away. I would never forget him.

Chapter 28

It was really cold when I arrived at Angela's that Thanksgiving Day. Jaylen and Jeremy had no idea I would be there. They thought I would be gone at least another week. When I got to her house, I hid in a room and waited for them to all come into the living room. When they were all there and had turned their backs to me, I came out of the room. When they turned around and saw me, they screamed with excitement.

"Mom!" they both said, running to me. Jaylen picked me up and swung me around. Once I landed, Jeremy grabbed me around the waist, laid his head on my stomach, and cried. Of course, I was crying, too. I was so happy to see them. After we got ourselves together emotionally, we sat down for dinner. It felt so good being back with the boys, but I wondered what Mike was doing. I missed him so much.

"So, Mom, did you see Sadaam Hussein?" Jeremy asked.

"No, he's in prison. I did get to go see where they were holding him, though."

"You did?" he asked, amazed. "Wow, I'm glad the bad guys didn't hurt you."

"Me too, Jeremy. I was lucky to be in a good location, but nobody is really safe."

"Were there any men over there?" Angela asked.

"Were there? Girl, they were coming out of the woodworks."

"Well?"

"Well, what?"

"Did you find any prospects?"

"Angela, I did not go over there looking for no man, ok?"

"Sara, how long are you going to keep punishing yourself? You need to find you somebody to keep you warm during those cold winters. Don't think every man out there is like Jacob. He was a low down, dirty dog and that other fella, he was just something to do. It will do you good to start going out again. Enjoy your life and stop staying stuck up in that house. We all make bad choices sometimes, but we learn from them. Look at you. You have already defeated the odds. I am so proud of you. You have come so far. You took the impossible and made it possible. You have blossomed into a beautiful woman. It's about time you see that. I want to see you happy, Sara, that's all."

"I am happy. Why does everybody think I'm unhappy just because I don't have a man?"

"Sara, when was the last time you got laid? You can't be happy."

"Angela, don't you see these kids at the table?"

"They want you to get laid, too, we have already had this conversation."

I was so embarrassed. She was right though, it had been a long time. I did want to be with a man, but I couldn't trust them anymore.

"Vanessa, will you come in here and help me out?" I yelled. Vanessa was also doing well. She worked as a doctor's assistant at a nearby Veterans Association Hospital. She was the baby of the family and spoiled rotten.

"I'm sorry, Sara," Vanessa said, coming into the kitchen where we were eating. "I agree with Angela. You got to start getting out. If you want me to, I can hook you up with one of my friends!"

"Ya'll are unbelievable and if you must know, I did meet someone."

"Uh oh, uh oh," Vanessa said, dancing around the table. "Is he cute?"

"A Mandingo!"

"Now, that's what I'm talking about. So, when are ya'll gonna hook up?"

"We not."

"What?" she asked as she stopped dancing.

"Can we eat, please? I don't want to talk about my Latin love."

"What, a Latino? You go, girl. You know they love them some brown sugar. He gonna treat you right. Yeah, you go ahead on and eat 'cause we got some talking to do after this."

"Will somebody pass me the potato salad?" I asked, glad that that part of our conversation was over, at least for the moment.

I enjoyed my time with my sisters. I always looked forward to spending time with them. I loved them so much. I was blessed to have them because they believed in me when I didn't believe in myself, and they always had my back no matter what.

I called Mama and let her know that I had made it back safely. I wished she and JaLisa was there, but I would see them in a couple of months along with Terrance and Marcus. They were still holding it down back home. When I thought about where we came from and where we were, all I could do was thank God. We beat the odds. We were not even close to what people predicted us to be. I was still not where I wanted to be, but I was glad I was not where I used to be.

Chapter 29

"Hey, Miss Shanna."

"Hey, Mom! Are you back?"

"Yep. I made it back again."

"Woo, thank You, Jesus. How are you doing?"

"I'm doing good, dreading going back to work."

"I know that's right. I want to come see you next weekend, is that ok?"

"Is that ok? That will be great. I have something to tell you, too."

"What is it? Did you go over there and find yourself a man? You did, didn't you?" she asked when I didn't answer right away.

"I will talk to you about it when you get here, ok?"

"I can't believe you're going to make me wait."

"I love you. I just wanted to call and let you know I made it back."

"Ah man, ok. I'll see you next week."

"Talk to you later."

♫♪♫♪♫♪♫♪

"Welcome back!" was the greeting I got from all my coworkers when I returned to work. I was there in body only; my mind and heart were still in Kuwait.

"Hey, everybody," I said, trying to sound excited.

"How was it over there? Is it as bad as the news say it is?" one of the girls asked.

"It was good. Depending on where you are, determines how good it is. Some places are a lot worse than others. I am just glad I made it back safely."

"Me too. I will be glad when everybody comes home," she said.

"We missed you, girl. We were worried about you. It seems like every day there was another fallen soldier. It is so good to see you," another girl said, giving me a hug.

I hugged her back and went to my desk. It didn't take me long to get back into the swing of things. Nothing changed while I was gone. After a while, it seemed like I never even left.

♫♪♫♪♫♪♫♪

"Hey, Shanna," Jaylen said, giving her a hug.

"Hey, guys," she said, taking off her coat. "Mom, it's cold. I didn't think it got that cold here."

"It depends on what part of the state you live in. Come on in and make yourself at home."

"I tried to get Grandma to come with me but she said maybe next time."

"Yeah, maybe next time," I said, knowing Mama didn't like traveling.

"Jeremy, you are getting so tall. How old are you now?"

"Thirteen," he said with a big ole grin.

"Ooh, listen to your voice, you sound like a man! Man, I can't believe you are getting ready for high school. Boy, I feel old."

"You can feel old all you want to, I ain't never getting old," I teased.

"Mom, you look great. When I show pictures of you, people think you are my sister."

"Why, thank you," I said, blushing.

"Sis, I'll be leaving soon," Jaylen said, joining in the conversation.

"I heard. I wish you'd do like I did and go to college first. I love being in charge."

"Didn't I tell you?" I said. "It's much better when you give orders instead of taking them, plus, you make more money."

"I thought about it, but I wanna be a sailor first and eventually become a Navy Seal. If I do well, then maybe I'll cross over."

"A Navy Seal? You better start training now. That's going to be tough, but I know you can do it. You're in good shape."

"I hope so. I've been hitting the gym. I'll know soon enough."

We ate dinner and were getting settled for the night. "Shanna, you wanna watch me play a game?" Jeremy asked.

"In a little while, Jeremy, I have to talk to Mom about something first."

"I'll play with you, Jeremy," Jaylen said.

"Cool," Jeremy said, happily.

Shanna followed me into my room. "Well, Mom, tell me what happened."

"Nothing really."

"What? You made me wait all this time to tell me nothing happened?"

"Well it did, but it didn't."

"Now you're confusing me. Why don't you just spit it out?"

"I did meet someone while I was down range."

"Good for you."

"Hold on. He was the most intriguing man I have ever met. We hit it off really well, but I wouldn't allow myself to have an intimate relationship with him."

"Why?"

"Why? Because I didn't just want to have a fling."

"I know what you mean, Mom, but I know folks who've met people down range and they are still together."

"I know, but I was afraid to take that chance. Shanna, have you ever been hurt by what you thought was love?"

"Un uh."

"It's not a good feeling, and I don't ever want to feel that way again."

"Who says you will? You will never find out if you don't step out on faith. You can't assume every man is like Dad. I can see why you would feel that way, but he was a jerk. I love him, but I don't like the way he treated you. You are a beautiful woman who deserves to be loved. I want to see you happy. You say you are, but I know deep down inside you're not."

"He was so nice. I have never met anyone like him," I said, reminiscing.

"If he left that kind of impression on you, you better look him back up."

"We keep in touch, but he doesn't know how I really feel."

"Well, you know, tomorrow is not promised. Even if you're happy for a little while, it's better than not at all. Let this man know how you feel. If he makes *you* happy, then we are all happy."

"I'll think about it. I'll let you know how things go."

"I wish you the best," she said.

"Thanks, now go in there and watch your brother play his game."

♫♪♫♪♫♪♫♪

Every day after work I followed the same routine. Helped Jeremy with his homework, watched TV, and went to bed. Boring was an understatement. I had absolutely nothing to look forward to. It was so cold, I didn't want to go anywhere. I hadn't talked to my girl, Tiffany, since I got back. I knew she was going to kill me for taking so long to call her. I had been back well over a month and if she knew I was back that long and hadn't called, she'd be quite upset. I thought I would have forgotten about Mike by now, but he was constantly on my mind. He had already emailed me and sent me an e-card letting me know he was thinking about me. He just didn't know how much I thought about him. I knew if I talked to Tiff she'd help me put things into perspective.

"Hello, Tiffany?"

"Hey, Sara!" she said with excitement. "When did you get back?"

I knew she was going to ask. "Not too long ago. How have you been?"

"Everything is good. I am glad you made it back safe. How was it?"

Why does everybody ask the same question? "It was ok. I'm glad to be back." That was partially true. I was glad to be back with the boys, but a part of me still wanted to be back in Kuwait.

"I will be coming that way soon, and when I find out exactly when, I'll let you know so I can stop by."

"I hope so, I ain't seen yo' butt in so long," I said.

"I know. How have you been?"

"I'm doing good, getting back into the swing of things. I got to get up out of here soon and go where it's warm. It's been snowing a lot lately. I hate being confined."

"I know what you mean. Are you dating anybody yet?"

I guess I am the only person in the world who ain't got nobody. "No, not yet."

"Girl, what are you waiting on? Don't let life pass you by."

"How 'bout I met this guy in Kuwait and fell madly in love with him?"

"No, you didn't?"

"Yes, I did. He don't know it, though."

"What? Why not?"

"Tiff, if I had gone over there and started something, it would have been just a temporary thrill."

"What's wrong with that? A temporary thrill is better than no thrill at all."

"Yeah, but you know I stopped sleeping around a long time ago."

"What he look like?"

Why are looks so important? That's always the first question. "Girl, he got it going on, and check this out, he's Mexican."

"What? You know what they say about them Latin lovers."

"No, what?"

"They love to do it."

"You crazy."

"They do. Why do you think they have a lot of children? I also heard they take care of their women. How many of them do you see in divorce court?"

"Tiff, he was soooo nice to me. He gave me a Swarovski Crystal angel. A part of me didn't want to come home."

"Now, this man got to be all that if you didn't want to come home. You sure you didn't give him some punany?"

"No, I didn't, but I wanted to the night he gave me the angel."

"Well, what you gonna do, girl?"

"I don't know. I still have his email address. We keep in contact, but reality is, he is there and I am here. That was our time and I blew it. An opportunity like that only comes once."

"Sara, you never know. If I were you, I'd be on that email right now letting his ass know how I felt."

"But, Tiff, what are the odds of me seeing him again?"

"I don't know, but you'll never find out if you don't try. You have never given up on anything. You are the strongest woman I know. If you want that man, go get him. How are the kids doing?"

"Good. Jaylen will be joining the Navy this spring."

"Really? I am glad he's joining the Navy. I heard they get treated good."

"I know. I'm proud of him. That will be two down and one to go."

"When is the last time you heard from Shanna?"

"Last night, she'll be going back over soon."

"Man, I tell you. I'll be glad when this war is over. Sara, is this your home number that showed up on the caller ID?"

"Uh huh."

"Ok. I'm going to program it into the phone. I'll be in touch. I got to go. Derrick is in there waiting for me to rock his world. The next time I talk to you, I hope it's good news with you and your Latin lover."

      "Maybe. Have fun."

      "Believe me, I will."

      "Love you."

      "Love you, too, bye."

Chapter 30

The time had come for Jaylen to leave. It was his time to go out into the world and make his mark. I hoped I taught him well because this world was a cruel, cruel place.

"Son, remember, it's going to be tough at first, but it's all a mind game. Just do what you're told and you'll be ok. You got Johnson blood running through your veins. I know you can handle it."

"I know, Mom. I will use you as my inspiration. I will call you as soon as I get a chance. I love you." He bent down and gave me a hug.

"I love you, too, son," I said, trying to be strong.

"Jeremy, you're the man of the house now. Can you handle it?"

"You know I can, Jaylen. You just don't let them scare you too bad."

"Who, me? Please," he said as they hugged each other.

"Ok, it's time to go," the recruiter said. I waved goodbye as I watched my son walk out of sight. I had a lump in my throat so big I couldn't swallow. He was gone. He was a man now. All I could do was pray for him.

♫♪♫♪♫♪♫♪

It seemed like every time I turned around, my boss wanted to send me somewhere. I didn't mind as long as Jeremy was taken care of, which was a major problem. Since Jaylen left, I really felt the single parent syndrome. I had been one for years, but was just starting to feel it. Now that it was just the two of us, it was getting harder to do the things I used to do. There was not a soul he could stay with when I was gone for days at a time. I felt the pressure from my boss when I had to turn down several trips, but he simply didn't understand. I wanted to do a good job at work, but I also wanted to be a good mom. I was really considering getting out of the military because of it, but since I had come this far, with God's help, I knew He would take me the rest of the way.

"Hey, Cheryl," I said, calling her one day after work.

"Hey, girl. What you up to?"

"Nothing much, just getting sick of this job."

"Oh yeah? What's going on?"

"They want to keep sending me on these trips and it's hard for me now since Jaylen left."

"Where are they trying to send you now? You just got back from Kuwait."

"Everywhere. The funny thing about it is when I wanted to go, they didn't have the funds and now that I can't, every time a trip comes up, my name is the first name out of their mouth. I don't mind the trips, I just don't have proper care for Jeremy when I'm gone. I will have him well after this job is gone. If Jacob was any count, I could send Jeremy to stay with him for a while, but I ain't even going to go there."

"You right about that. How much longer do you have there?"

"I don't know. I think we have to do three years. I've only been here a year and a half."

"Keep praying, chile. God is faithful."

"I know. I wouldn't have made it this far without Him. What's going on with you?"

"Not a lot, working every day as usual. When is Jaylen graduating?"

"Next week. I don't get to talk to him much, they got him strung out."

"I know that's right," she said, laughing. "I sure wish I could go with you. If I had known it was that soon, I would have put in for leave. You did a good job with those kids, Sara. You have stuck by them through thick and thin."

"Yeah, and when I get old, they gon' put me in a rest home," I said, laughing.

"You and me both."

"Alright, girl, I just wanted to holla."

"Ok, love you."

"Love you, too. Bye."

Jaylen looked so good at his graduation. He had changed so much over the last couple of months. He had gotten much bigger and had more discipline. It was a shame Jacob didn't come out and support him, but it was his loss.

"Congratulations, son!"

"Thanks," he said, smiling.

"It seems like just yesterday you were at my graduation. Now look at you. Man, how time flies."

"I know. It was a lot tougher than I thought, but I hung in there."

"I knew you could do it. You have made me so proud."

"Jeremy, you been taking care of the house?"

"Yep," he said proudy.

"Yeah, he's doing a good job."

"Ok. I'm depending on you."

"I ain't helpless, Jaylen." I said defensively.

"I know, but you can't do everything by yourself," he said, throwing his arm across my shoulder.

"I don't know where they're sending me yet. I hope I can go to Japan."

"Are you sure you want to go there on your first assignment?"

"Yeah, I heard it was a good tour."

"If that's what you want, son, go for it."

"I'm gonna try. Nothing is guaranteed."

"Tomorrow is not guaranteed."

"Let's go get something to eat and I'm treating!" he said proudly.

We got something to eat, took pictures, gave kisses and hugs, said our goodbyes, and me and Jeremy flew back to Maryland. I may have failed in a lot of areas, but I did right by my kids. *Thank You, Jesus.*

Chapter 31

Time was moving on for everybody but me. I was still in the same place I was in a year ago. Not after today, though. Life was too short. I was going to write my baby. I didn't know what had happened since we last talked, which was some time ago, but I was not waiting any longer. I hoped he had not gotten married. If he had, she was a lucky woman. I guess as the old saying goes, 'If you snooze, you lose.' I hoped that was not true in my case. There was only one way to find out:

Hi Mike,

I hope this email finds you in good health and you are doing well. It has been a while, but I haven't forgotten about you and I don't think I ever will. I am doing well and so is the family. Shanna is in her third year of college and Jaylen just graduated Naval basic training. I am so proud of him. He is my "young man" now. Jeremy has assumed the role of the man of the house; so far so good. I am still here in Maryland awaiting orders to my next assignment. I was just thinking about you and wanted to say hi. When you get the chance, write me back. It will be good to hear from you.

Sara

Well, Lord, I hope he answers me back. I really miss him and our conversations. Only time will tell.

It had been a couple of days since I emailed Mike and I had heard nothing. I guess I waited too late. What did I expect? It *had* been close to a year. I knew he had moved on by now. I did hope he was doing ok.

Lately, since I had a lot of time on my hands, I had enrolled back into college, and was taking my classes online. At least I had gotten my associates degree. It was going to take a lot for me to get my bachelors. I hoped I could accomplish that before I left the military. I had been working on a class when my email notifier said,

"You've got mail." *I hope it's Mike*, I said to myself as I slowly opened my mailbox. "Yes! It's him!" I said excitedly.

Hey Beautiful,

I thought you had forgotten me. What a pleasant surprise to find your email. I am doing fine and glad that you are, too. I still remember the first time we met. It was one of the best days of my life. I have been really thinking about you and would love to see you again. I always meet the right person at the wrong time. Well, Sweetie, it's my pleasure to write. Take care of yourself. One day our paths are going to cross. Until I hear from you, take care.

Mike

Ooh, baby, baby, ooh, baby, baby. Yessss! I am going to write him back right now. I am not letting him get away from me again.

Hi Mike.

It was great hearing from you. I am glad you are doing ok. I have been thinking about you ever since I left Kuwait, especially our coffee dates, and I truly miss them. I was so afraid of relationships at the time, but I don't want to spend the rest of my life by myself. Don't get me wrong, I've enjoyed my 'me time' but to meet someone and it feels so right only happens once in a lifetime. I never felt safer with anyone than I felt with you. I would really like to pursue this as a relationship, if you're not already involved or married, and if you say no because of the distance, I understand. I still want to let you know that you made an impact on my life, and I'll never forget you no matter what, but you deserve to know how I really feel. You only go around once in life. You take care of yourself, and I hope to hear from you soon.

Sara

Sara,

I, too, miss our coffee dates. I truly understand your situation in Kuwait, and I only hope you saw that I had the utmost respect for you. I never once tried to get you in bed. I knew better. You were a classy woman and deserved that respect. Sara, this is a dream come true. If the distance is not an issue, I think we can make this happen. I would love to spend time with you. Any sane man would be crazy not to. I am so excited about this relationship, and can't wait to see your beautiful face. Speaking of beautiful, if you have any pictures, I would love to have some. I could never get tired of looking at you. They will simply remind me of the beautiful woman I have waiting for me. Well, sexy, I have to go now. I have changed jobs since you left, and this one is really demanding, but I hope you have a good night, and I look forward to your next email.

Mike

Mike and I continued to correspond over the next several months. We talked about any and everything. I let him know what I was looking for in the relationship and he let me know what he was looking for. We were a good match. I told him some of the things I'd gone through and assured him I would not let that reflect in our relationship, but I did ask for his patience. I was beginning to feel like I had known him all my life. He made me laugh all the time and for the first time, I was beginning to experience real love. Who said you have to have sex to be in love? Not true. That man was already part owner of my heart and we had never had sex. I could not wait to see him again. I knew he would be coming home soon and I was so excited. I sent him the pictures he had asked for and the more I sent, the more he wanted. It was my pleasure because for the first time in my life, I truly felt cared about.

Hey Gorgeous,

In two weeks, we will be in each other's arms. I hope you are ready for me because I am definitely ready for you. I have waited months for this moment. I cannot wait to gaze into your beautiful eyes, to hold you in my arms, and kiss you all over and cap the night off by making passionate love to you. You are definitely a dream come true, and I don't want to lose you again. I would still like to fly you to Miami, if that's ok? I want to show you how I treat my woman. I am about to make reservations, and just want to make sure things are going as planned. Ok, sexy, the countdown is on. I will send you the flight info as soon as I get everything confirmed. Stay sweet, baby. Talk to you soon :)

Mike

Hey Sweetie,

I would love to meet you in Miami. I have also waited for this opportunity for such a long time. I know it's going to be a dream come true. If you liked me in Kuwait, you can only love me here. These past few months have been the best ever. Getting your emails has given me something to look forward to. I can't wait to see my baby. I am so excited. I don't feel like I'm walking, I feel like I'm floating. You are always on my mind. I know we are going to have a good time together. Be safe, baby. It is just a matter of time now. Talk to you soon.

Sara

Chapter 32

"Hello?"

"Hey, Tiff."

"Hey. What's up?"

"Nothing much, just anxious. Are you still going to be able to keep Jeremy for me?"

"Ahh, yeah. I didn't change my mind. I can keep him as long as you need me to."

"Thanks. Mike will be in on Wednesday and I want to bring Jeremy by tomorrow night. I am glad they have a couple of days off from school. That way he won't miss but two days."

"Are you excited?"

"Excited is an understatement. I am so nervous. I haven't seen him in almost a year."

"I told you to email him. See how things turned out? You better loosen up, girl, and enjoy yourself. You've waited a long time for this moment. Have fun. Don't even think about Jeremy, he is in good hands."

"I know. Tiff, you're the best."

"I know. Now get off this phone and start packing. I know you got something sexy to wear, don't you?"

"I got two negligees. After that, he will be seeing me in my birthday suit."

"Rock his world, girl. Make him want to keep coming back."

"I plan on it. I'll see you tomorrow night."

"Ok, I'll be here. Sara, I am so happy for you. I don't think I've ever seen you so happy. I can't wait to meet the man who was able to tear down that wall you built around your heart. Have a good time, girl."

"Thanks, girl. I will. See you tomorrow."

♪♪♪♪♪♪♪♪♪

"Are you sure you're only going to be gone for a few days?" Jeremy asked as he was putting a few last minute things into his suitcase.

"Just for a few days. Make sure you take your cell phone and charger so I can call you."

"I will. I want you to have a good time. I will be fine at Tiff's, so don't worry about me. Me and Terrell will be playing games and watching TV."

"Good. I'm glad to hear that. I am going to have a good time and if all goes well, maybe one day soon you will get to meet him."

"As long as he treats you right, I'm happy."

"Me too," I said, giving him a big squeeze. "You ready to go?"

"Yes, ma'am."

"Ok, let's hit it. We got a long drive ahead of us."

It was late when I got to Tiff's, so I got Jeremy settled in and spent the night. I got up early the next morning, kissed Jeremy on the forehead, gave Tiff a big thank you hug, and started on my way. Once I got back, I started packing for myself. I would soon be leaving to meet my prince. I was so excited, I could hardly sleep. He was all I thought about. It was a dream becoming reality, a dream I didn't want to wake up from. It seemed like an eternity, but I would soon be with my baby, the man I ran from a year earlier. I could not wait to be in his arms.

Hey Beautiful,

I finally made it to the states and talking about a long trip. Whew. I'm glad it's over. I will be taking the last leg of the trip in about an hour. I will phone you from the hotel. I can't wait to hear your voice. I sure wish I could take you back with me. Talk to you soon, baby.

Truly excited

I was just putting the last few items in the suitcase when the phone rang. "Hello!"

"Hey, beautiful."

"Hey, baby! How are you?" I asked, grinning from ear to ear.

"I'm good, girl. How is my baby doing?" he asked.

"Fine, now. It's so good to hear your voice. It has been so long," I said excitedly.

"I know. Baby, I cannot wait to see you. What time are you leaving for the airport?"

"In two hours. I am already packed just waiting for the taxi. How was your flight?"

"It was rough. I could not get comfortable, but it was all worth it because I know who I will be sleeping with tonight."

"Baby, you sound so good. I can't wait to hold you."

"Me neither. You are so beautiful, you know that? You sure you don't want to go back with me?"

"I wish. I want to spend every minute I can with you."

"You don't have to worry about that. We are definitely going to get to know each other. What do you want for dinner tonight?"

"Anything but shellfish. I used to eat it, but something happened along the way and now I'm allergic to it."

"Oh yeah, that's right. I'll make sure I get everything but. Ok, babe, I got a couple of things I need to do before I pick you up at the airport. Don't you dare miss your flight."

"That is one thing you don't have to worry about. I wouldn't miss it for the world."

"Ok, baby, I'll see you in a few hours."

"Ok, see you soon."

♫♪♫♪♪♫♪♫♪

I could not wait to get in that taxi. It usually took about thirty minutes to get to the airport but traffic was thick since it was getting close to quitting time. It would only take two and a half hours to get to my baby. I could only imagine how it was going to be when we were finally together. I hoped he was good at lovemaking because I was long overdue for some good loving. I didn't want to get any sleep that night, just some pure loving; loving my baby all night long.

"Excuse me, sir, is there an alternate route? We have been sitting here for close to five minutes."

"Well, ma'am, if we can get up the road another mile or so, we can take the carpool lane. We should be able to make up our time. It must have been an accident or something, traffic isn't usually this bad."

"Just my luck."

"What time does your flight leave?"

"In an hour and a half, but you know how hard it is getting through security. I really don't want to miss my flight."

"I'll get you there in time."

"Let's hope so. That's the last flight for today." I could not bear the thought of not seeing my baby tonight. I was beginning to get nervous. If I could, I would have got out and ran. I would probably get there faster.

We did get there just in the nick of time. As soon as I checked my bag, went through security, and got to my gate, they were calling for all first class passengers. That would be me. My baby was flying me first class. He said I deserved nothing but the best and said he would give me nothing less. It was really hard for me to believe I was being treated that way. I came from not amounting to nothing to flying first class. What a way to go. I loved that man already and I hardly knew him.

The flight took off on time and I was really on my way. I took plenty of reading material to keep me occupied, but I was too excited to read. I could feel the perspiration roll from under my arm. I knew I had better check my deodorant. The last thing I wanted was to show up smelling like mustard. "Ladies and gentlemen, we are now starting our descent, please raise your seats to their upright positions..."

This is it. Time for me to see my baby. I hope I still look good to him. I would hate to disappoint him and this whole trip turn out to be a disaster. After we deplaned and walked through that long tunnel to the airport, people were all over the place waiting for their loved ones or whomever it was they were there to meet. I didn't see Mike anywhere. Boy, I hoped he didn't play me. Where was he?

"Looking for me?" I heard a familiar voice from behind me say. I turned around to see my baby standing there looking as handsome as ever.

"I sure am," I said, dropping my bag to give him a hug. I know we hugged for fifteen seconds.

"Turn around and let me look at you," he said, taking my hand and turning me around. "Baby, you still look good. I never saw you in civilian clothes. You are hot."

"Thank you, baby. You look good yourself."

He pulled me to him and planted a kiss on my lips. I mean, a kiss. For the first time, I tasted his tongue and it tasted so good. I could not wait to get more. My body was starting to show signs of desire and at that moment, he could have had me right there on the spot.

"Here, these are for you," he said, handing me a bouquet of flowers.

"They are beautiful, Mike. Thank you," I said, surprised.

"You're welcome, baby. Let's go get your bags. We got to get out of here. I have some plans for us tonight," he said.

"Oh, yeah. What?"

"Let's go. I'll show you."

We got into Mike's rental, a Nissan 350Z, and headed for the Radisson Hotel. He had gotten us a room on the fifteenth floor. He pulled in front of the hotel and popped the trunk of the car. The bellhop came over and got our bags. Mike handed the keys to another bellhop as he approached the car.

"When you want your car, Mr. Colón, just call the front desk. We'll make sure it is waiting for you when you come down."

"Thanks, I will." Mike told him and handed him a tip. I was living a fairytale. Somebody pinch me. I had to be dreaming. Mike grabbed my hand and we walked inside. The lobby was huge. It exuded the luxury and sophistication of any hotel I'd ever been in. It had exotic mahogany woods, imported marbles. The art décor and antiques created a fusion of elegance. We walked down a corridor which was mirrored on both sides toward the elevators.

"How do you like it so far?" Mike asked me as we waited for the elevator.

"I'm speechless. I have never seen anything so beautiful."

"The best is yet to come."

I looked at him, grabbed him around his waist, and laid my head on his chest. I didn't want to be any other place except where I was at that moment. When we got to our floor, we walked down the hall and turned a corner that held only two rooms. When he opened the door, it took everything in me not to cry. I couldn't see anything for the rose petals. There were red, pink, and yellow petals everywhere.

"Come on," Mike said as he pulled me into the room. I looked to my left and there was a forty two inch flat screen TV mounted on the wall. When I looked to my right, there was a giant king sized bed with a white comforter turned down and a single red rose lying on the pillow.

"One more thing," he said, pulling back a curtain I thought led to a terrace. "What do you think?" I could not believe the hotel had a six jet Jacuzzi. "Baby, remember I said I wanted a tub big enough for the both of us? Do you think this one is big enough?"

At that point, I just started crying. I could not hold the tears back any longer. "Baby, this is the most amazing thing I've ever seen in my life. I could only dream about something like this. My life started out so badly. People had low expectations of me. I had low expectations of myself. I allowed myself to be treated so badly and I never in a million years thought this would be happening to me. I feel like I'm living somebody else's dream."

"No, baby, this is not a dream. When I met you I knew you were special and I wanted you from day one. I have met many women in my life, but something about you was calling out to me. The way you carried yourself, you were so confident and so classy, I knew I wanted to be a part of your life and when you left me, my world collapsed. You don't know how happy I was to get your email. I thought about you every day. I prayed for the day I'd be able to hold you in my arms and now that I have you, I don't ever want to let you go." He bent over and kissed me again. It was so tender and passionate, I didn't want it to end. "Baby, I want to do something special for you tonight. Do you think an hour is enough time to get dressed to go somewhere nice?"

"Yeah, as long as you don't take too long in the bathroom," I said, teasing.

"Me? You're the one who is going to take forever. You know how you ladies are. Let me go in first, ok?"

"Ok. I'll see if I can find a good jazz station on the radio."

"Ok, see you in a few," he said, giving me a small kiss on the lips.

Mike went into the shower as I marveled at the room. I found a good station on the radio and went out to the terrace to look at the view. I went through my suitcase and got out an elegant blue dress that accentuated my breasts, hips, and butt. It stopped just above the knees and clung to my body like a glove. I knew he would like to see me in it. He was in and out the bathroom in fifteen minutes. He came out with a T-shirt and shorts on. "Do you think you can beat that time, baby?"

"I don't know, but I'll be looking good when I come out." I grabbed my bag and went in the bathroom. I gave him a kiss and told him, "I'll see you in a few."

"Ok, I'll see you in an hour," he joked.

I was in the bathroom for about thirty-five minutes. I had to dry off and let some of the steam out before I could lotion up and put on my makeup. When I walked out, I wanted to look like a million bucks.

Mike called softly, "Baby, you coming out tonight?"

"Yeah," I said, opening the door feeling confident about how I looked.

When I turned the corner, all I could see was a table fit for a king. All the lights were off except the two lighted candles burning on the tables, which emitted enough light for me to see the table and my prince sitting down waiting for me. Dinner by candlelight, he was so romantic. The jazz music was playing softly in the background and rose petals were on the table.

"Baby, you look stunning," he said, staring at me. He was dressed in a grey, single breasted, four-button suit with a white shirt and a black, silver, and mauve Italian silk necktie.

"Uh uh, baby, you look like you just stepped out of a *GQ* magazine. How did you do all this?" I asked, referring to the table.

"Room service. I saw the menu earlier today and I wanted to do something special for you without going out. I know you had a long day and I wanted you to relax, plus, I wanted you all to myself tonight." He got up from the table and came around to pull my chair out for me.

"Baby, this is lovely. What's on the menu?"

"Here, let me," he said as he started uncovering all the dishes. "First, we have T-bone steak with your choice of steak sauce. Then, we have stuffed baked potatoes. Next, we have some cheesy broccoli and some whole wheat rolls. Your salad comes with balsamic vinaigrette dressing, and for dessert, we have cheesecake with a drizzle of cherry sauce, and, last but not least, who could resist the sensual allure of a bowl of chocolate covered strawberries? Here, allow me," he said as he poured me a chilled glass of Moet.

"Baby, you outdid yourself. Wait a minute. I want to take a picture of this." I went and got my camera out of my purse. I set the timer so that we could get in along with the table. I never wanted to forget that moment.

Mike and I ate and talked. We were so glad to be in each other's company. The chemistry between us was great, but I already knew that from being with him in Kuwait. That was why we went out for coffee so much. I never saw him in anything but T-shirts and shorts. Now, here he was wearing a single breasted suit gazing into my eyes. If this wasn't heaven I didn't know what was.

"So, baby, did you get enough?"

"Oh yeah, I'm stuffed. The food was delicious, especially the steak. I am glad it wasn't tough."

"Me too. I started to order something else for the exact reason, but I think they did a good job. I am satisfied." Well, he had more satisfaction coming up. He was not going to be completely satisfied until I got finished with him.

Mike called room service and they came and got the table. We still kept the candles burning because we liked the aura they were transmitting. "Mike, if we're not going anywhere, I would like to change into something more comfortable."

"Me too. Go ahead and change. I've got to go to the bathroom." I went to my suitcase to pick out some shorts when Mike called me, "Baby?"

"Yes?" I called back, moving closer to the bathroom so I could hear better.

"Can you come in here for a minute?"

I went into the bathroom to see what he wanted. Here was this man, six feet, two hundred and thirty pounds, standing in front of me in his birthday suit, and damn did he look good. I was mesmerized by what I saw dangling between his legs. I had no idea my baby was swinging like that. I was still staring when he grabbed me by the hand and pulled me into the bathroom. "Baby, I've waited a long time for this moment. Will you take this shower with me?" he whispered as he unbuttoned my dress.

I didn't say a word. All I could do was look at his body standing in front of me and the erection that had my name written all over it. I had no doubt I was going to get satisfied in a few minutes. After I got my clothes off, Mike gazed at my body, picked me up, and took me to the shower, kissing me all the way. I sure hoped he liked what he saw because this was me. I was content with my body, I hoped he liked it. He lathered me up from head to toe. He started with my arms, then my back, and when he got to my breasts, he lingered a while. He bent over and put one in his mouth. It didn't take long for my body to respond. While he had that one in his mouth, he started caressing the other one. I started to moan. I took my hand and put it on his Johnson and started caressing it. That was when he started to moan.

"Baby," he said. "I have waited for this for months. I want to treat you like the queen you are. Are you sure you are ready?"

"Baby, I am past ready. I, too, have been waiting. I thought I had lost you forever. You got my body craving your love and yes, I want you to make love to me. I want you to make love to me right now."

Mike took his hand and put it between my legs. He moved it back and forth a few times before he slid his finger inside. "Oh, baby, you feel so good,"

I continued to stroke his Johnson until it became rock hard. I knew it was going to be pure pleasure when he put it inside me. Mike pushed the shower head toward the wall and squatted down between my legs. He lifted one leg and put it on the edge of the tub. When his hot tongue touched my hot spot, I jumped. He grabbed me around my waist and pulled me closer to him. He licked my kitty to the point where I thought I was going to lose my mind. I rubbed his head and moaned loudly because this was pure ecstasy.

"Ooh, baby, this feels so good," I moaned. "Yes, baby, that's my spot, baby, that's my spot."

Mike didn't say a word. The only thing he had on his mind was satisfying me and he was definitely doing that. He took both of his hands and parted my lips. He licked and he sucked. At that point, I was gyrating my hips to his rhythm and I knew at any moment I was going to explode. Mike stood up, cut the water off, and got out of the tub. He picked me up and carried me to the bed. He laid me down and put his head right back between my legs. He was a professional at what he was doing because in no time at all, I was cumming, and boy, did I cum. Mike pulled himself up on top of me. He reached into the drawer and pulled out a condom.

"Wait a minute, baby, it's my turn. Lay down," I said to him, feeling confident about what I was about to do.

Mike lay down and I went to the bottom of the bed. *I hope I can take all this in my mouth*, I said to myself. *This is not a little man.* I took my tongue and teased the head. I licked his Johnson like it was a lollipop. Then, I took my tongue and played with the tip. He was moaning, squirming, and pulling my hair. I slid my tongue up and down his shaft until it was good and wet. Then, I took him completely in my mouth, squeezing my jaws as I moved vigorously up and down.

"Ohh, baby," he moaned loudly. "What are you doing to me? Oooh, it feels so good. Oh, girl, uh uh uh."

Mike was squeezing my arms, my back, and my shoulders. He was moaning so loudly I thought we were going to get a knock on the door. I was working my mouth like it was second nature. I was there to satisfy my baby, and that was what I was doing. Thank God for those 'fun parties'.

"Oh, baby," he said as I moved my head up and down. I took my hand and put it on the base of his love tool, and stroked it a few times up and down, and then put it back in my mouth. That drove him crazy. "I'm about to cum, baby. I'm about to cum," he moaned, grabbing me tightly.

"Cum, baby, cum," I said, letting my hand do all the work now.

"Here it comes, baby." When he said that, he skeeted all over me. I still kept working his Johnson with my hand until he had stopped cumming.

"Baby, where have you been all my life?" he asked as we lay cuddling, recovering from round one.

"Right here, waiting for you."

"I want to show you the world. I am not going to be over there much longer. I just want to make sure I make enough money to send my kids to college and secure my future, or should I say our future. After that, I am coming to get my baby. Will you be willing to wait for me?"

"If you keep treating me like this, I can wait a lifetime."

"Good, because I don't want to live my life without you." He turned over and started kissing me. I could feel his nature starting to rise again. He reached over and grabbed the condom.

"Let me," I said, taking the condom from him. I opened the wrapper and put it on his erect Johnson. He continued to kiss me as I took his love tool and guided it between my legs into my already pulsating sweet spot. He entered me slowly as he looked at me ever so sexily. I was in love with that man. He had so much passion to give. He stroked me for a good forty five minutes. He turned me every which way but loose, and I enjoyed every minute of it. He was the perfect fit. He had satisfied me in every possible way a man could satisfy a woman. He definitely knew how to lick a kitty. He was the total package.

♫♪♫♪♫♪♫♪♫

We made love all throughout the night and into the morning. Thank God for condoms. My kitty was completely satisfied. Mike got up before I did and went to run water in the Jacuzzi. I was tired. He had worn me out. He came over to the bed and said, "I know this will relax you." He grabbed me by the hand and led me to the Jacuzzi. It was filled with rose scented bubbles. Since all I had on was a T-shirt, getting undressed took all of two seconds. "Get in, baby," he said, still holding my hand. I stepped in the tub and the temperature of the water was just right. Mike stepped in behind me. "I want you to lay down on my chest and relax."

I laid my back against his chest and it felt so good. We laid there, talked, and locked our hands together as the warm water ran down our arms. He took the sponge and squeezed the water onto my back and kissed it ever so softly. He sucked on my shoulders and then my ears. The temperature was beginning to rise as I turned over and kissed him passionately. I straddled him and sat on his joy stick.

"I thought I was going to relax, baby," I whispered, moving my body slowly up and down, enjoying the ride.

"I can't get enough of you," he said, holding me around my waist.

I rode him until I heard him sigh, and I knew he was cumming when he squeezed me to him. After a while, we got out, Mike dried me off, and carried me back to the bed.

"I'm only going to lay here for a few minutes," I said as he pulled the covers over me.

"You lay there as long as you like, beautiful. You are on vacation, right? We can go somewhere later on. Just relax and enjoy yourself."

"I am, baby. I've enjoyed every minute of being here."

"I'm glad. I want you to. Nothing makes me happier than pleasing you. I'll be right back." Mike went into the bathroom and when he came out, he was dressed in his usual.

"Room service," a voice called from the door.

"You're going to enjoy this, too. Come on in," Mike yelled to them as he opened the door. I slumped in the bed and pulled the covers over my head. I didn't want whoever it was to see me in my birthday suit. "Thank you very much," Mike said to the waiter as he left the room.

"Baby, you could have warned me."

"What? You look good, girl."

"Yeah right."

I attempted to get up to go join him when he said, "No, sexy. You stay right there. How do you like your coffee?"

"Just like you, sweet," I said.

"Ok, mi amor," he said, blushing. He brought my coffee over and sat it on the night stand. He then made me a plate of eggs, bacon, oatmeal, some fruit, and said, "Baby, raise up some." I rose up out of the bed. He brought the tray over and sat it on my lap. "I want you to have breakfast in bed this morning."

"Why, thank you, baby." I rose up and ate my breakfast. He came and got my tray and then sat on the foot of the bed. He reached under the covers and grabbed both my legs and put them in his lap. He started at my calves and massaged all the way down to my feet one leg at a time. That man never ceased to amaze me. Where did he come from? Was he real? After he finished his massage, I got up and got dressed.

We spent the day walking hand-in-hand along the beach, picking up sea shells and feeding the sea gulls. We had lunch in one of the store front cafes before heading back to the hotel. After taking a shower, we decided to go to the hotel lounge to have a drink.

"Can I get a cranberry juice and vodka, and a margarita for my lady? Make hers a double," Mike told the bartender.

"A double?" I asked, surprised. A double definitely would have me drunk, but I didn't care. I was with my baby. I knew I was safe with him.

We were in the bar for about two hours when we decided to go back to the room, and I was definitely feeling woozy. When we got there, we kicked off our shoes, turned on the jazz, and laid across the bed. It felt so good lying in his arms.

"Baby, do you know what I want?" he asked

"No, what?"

"Some more of that sweet potato pie."

"Oh yeah?"

"Uh huh. You're so hot and moist, all I'm missing is some whip cream."

"I think I can make the cream for you, baby," I said as I pulled him on top of me.

We made love again and again. I promise you he was the best lover I had ever had. Why? Because he took his time. He didn't just want to hit it and leave. He treated me like a queen and I would never look at myself any other way. He was my everything and I wished he didn't have to go back. A man like him only happened once in a lifetime. He was definitely the love of my life.

"Baby, I sure do hate I have to leave tomorrow."

"I think I hate it more than you do. I don't even want to think about it. I have had so much fun these last few days. I never want this to end."

"It won't, baby. I will be back before you know it. Here, I brought you something." He went in his bag and brought out a teddy bear. "I want you to have this. I know it doesn't compare to the angel I gave you, but when I saw it, I knew I wanted you to have it."

"Thank you, baby," I said, taking the bear. "I brought you something, too." I went into my purse and pulled out two necklaces. "This is a broken hearted necklace. I want you to take one half with you and I will keep the other half with me. One day, the hearts are going to be reunited. Do you want it?"

"Of course, I want it. Whenever I look at it, I'll be reminded of the angel who is holding the other half."

"I am so glad you came back. I feel so special. You could have spent your time with anyone, but you chose to spend it with me. I missed you so much when you were gone, but now, I have everything to look forward to."

"No, *I* have everything to look forward to."

"Mike, I want to take another picture of you. Wait right there." I went to the table and got my camera. I took two more pictures of my baby. "I will keep these forever."

"Let me take one of you."

"Baby, you got so many pictures of me already."

"I could never have enough pictures of you." So, he took a few more pictures of me.

♫♪♫♪♫♪♫♪

It seemed like that night went by in the blink of an eye. Before I knew it, it was time to take Mike to the airport. I was scheduled to fly out later that day.

"Baby, do you have your phone?" I asked as he was making sure he didn't forget anything.

"Yeah, I have it right here."

"Ok. I want you to call me as soon as you can. I know once you get overseas it's not going to work anymore, so call me the very last chance you get."

"I will, baby. Listen, I had a great time. You are so special. You see I am wearing the necklace," he said with a smile. "I will be back in a few months. I miss you already and I haven't even left yet. This was so much fun. I can't wait until we are together again."

"Me either. I have never experienced anything like this. You have made me so happy. I wish we had more time to spend together, but I know this is just temporary and one day soon, we will be together."

"Count on it, my beautiful brown sugar. I don't want to spend my life with anyone but you," he said, kissing me ever so tenderly. Room service came and picked up his bags. When we got downstairs, the car was waiting for us. We got to the airport so fast it seemed like it was right next door. I got out and helped him with his bags.

"It will only be a few months. Remember that," he said once he got all his bags.

"I know, baby. I will be here waiting for you."

"I'll call as soon as I can. See you soon."

We hugged for about five minutes. His kisses tasted like honey. He picked up his bags and headed to the door. Tears rolled down my face as I saw him walking away. He stopped and turned around. He blew me a kiss and motioned for me to leave. I pulled off with him watching me until I was out of sight. I had that same lump in my throat I felt when I didn't want to cry, but that time I did. I cried because my baby was gone again. Although it was only for a little while, it would feel like an eternity.

Chapter 33

That was the longest flight back ever. Not distance wise, but mentally. All I could think about was the fun I had those past few days. There was nothing anybody could say to me that would break my spirits. I had waited a very long time for someone to appreciate me, to love me for who I was, the person I'd always been. I didn't have to wait any longer; my knight in shining armor had arrived. It was a shame I had to go all the way to Kuwait to find him, talk about being in the right place at the right time. I was looking forward to the future and I was so glad that Mike would be a part of it.

"Hey, Tiffany. What's up?" I asked when the phone rang.

"Hey, you back?"

"Yeah, we just landed. Is everything ok?"

"Everything is fine. I just didn't know if it was so good that you decided to stay longer. Jeremy was good. He and Terrell played games most of the time. I did take them to the library, though. I told them it was going to take more than games to make it in this world. I made them jokers read. So, tell me what happened?"

"Tiff, I had the time of my life. He flew me to Miami and it was so romantic. The hotel looked like it could have been in the Trump Towers and it was right on the beach. When we got to our room, there were rose petals everywhere. We had dinner by candle light and breakfast in bed. Tiff, he could make some good love, girl. I felt like royalty."

"Wow, it sounds like something in a fairytale."

"I know. That's what I keep telling myself and it's hard to believe it happened to me."

"It's not hard for me to believe. Look at how long it took you to get back out on the dating scene. You took that time to get to know yourself and what you wanted. Some people never find themselves and will settle for anything. You deserve this and more. When am I going to get the chance to meet him?"

"He'll be back in six months... wait a minute, Tiff, I got a beep. Hello?"

"Hey, sexy, I was calling to check in before my flight took off."

"Hey. Hold on, baby." I clicked back over to Tiff. "Tiff, I'll finish telling you when I get there. That's him on the line," I said excitedly.

"Handle your business, girl. Bye."

I went back to Mike's line. "I'm back, baby. Where are you at now?"

"Atlanta. I will be taking off shortly. I keep looking at our pictures. Have I told you lately how beautiful you are?"

"Yes, all the time," I said, blushing.

"You are. How did I get so lucky?"

"Luck had nothing to do with it. It was destiny."

"Oh yeah?"

"You can't tell me otherwise. How else can you explain how we left each other over a year ago and found our way back into each other's arms? This was meant to be."

"I'll accept that. I am so glad you sent me that email. I really did miss you."

"I missed you, too, and I am not letting you get away from me again."

"You don't have to worry about that. I'm just glad you had a good time."

"I had a ball."

"It gets better and better. How about meeting me in Paris next summer?"

"I'll be there with bells on my toes."

"Well, gorgeous, I got to go. They just called for boarding. I will email or call you the first chance I get. I'll talk to you soon."

"Have a good trip, babe, and be safe."

"I will. Bye now."

After my flight landed and the taxi dropped me off at home, I went straight to Tiffany's to pick Jeremy up. I was glad he had a good time because I sure did. I could not stop smiling. I could feel Mike deep in my soul. When I looked over and saw the teddy bear, I grabbed it and squeezed it. I could still smell his scent on it and it brought such closeness. I could not get him off my mind.

"So, finish telling me. I know it must have been good because you've been glowing ever since you got here," Tiffany said after I arrived and got settled.

"Tiff, it was great. Did you see the movie *Pretty Woman?* I feel just like her. It was so magical. I have to keep pinching myself to make sure it's real. He picked me up in a sports car and the hotel was outta this world."

"Did you wear the negligees?"

"Not once. He was so passionate. We made love the whole time we were there. He even massaged my legs, girl, but do you know what I liked most about the whole trip?"

"What?"

"Our conversations. We never got tired of talking."

"You see? Didn't I tell yo' butt to email him? Now look at you, walking around here glowing and shit. Am I going to meet him when he comes back?"

"I don't know. He wants to fly me to Paris."

"Sara, I am so happy for you. It's about time. I wish ya'll the best," she said, giving me a hug.

"Thanks."

Chapter 34

Mike emailed when he got back letting me know he had a safe trip. I missed him terribly but knew he would be coming back soon. I had since told everybody about my four day rendezvous and they were all excited for me. They claimed they could hear a change in my voice when they talked to me on the phone. I had changed. Being with Mike did bring out the best in me. No matter how stressed out I got, talking to him always made me feel better. It seemed like he always knew the right things to say.

Things at work were the same. I still had to take trips, but I tried to go on the ones that would only require me to be gone for no more than two days at a time. Luckily Deborah, a girl at work, was able to keep Jeremy on those days. She was a big help and he enjoyed staying with her, but I knew I wanted a more stable life for him. Although he was a teenager and stood about five feet eight, he was still too young to stay home by himself.

It had been only weeks since Mike left, but it felt like forever. I missed waking up in his arms and feeling those baby soft hands of his in mine. I was glad we were able to talk every day and hearing his voice made it feel like he was right here with me.

"Mom, somebody is at the door!" Jeremy yelled from his room.

I opened the door to see a UPS truck pulling off and was surprised by the box he left. I hadn't ordered anything lately. What could it be? When I looked at the sender's name and saw that it was from Mike, I got excited. *He didn't tell me he was sending me anything.* I anxiously opened the box and what was inside blew my mind. A diamond bracelet and a note saying:

Hey beautiful,

Surprised, huh? I told you that you were my queen and that I was going to treat you as such. I really hope you like it. I was trying to find something as elegant as you are and this bracelet is just the beginning of things to come. You should be getting another package tomorrow or the next day. I will call you tonight. Take care!

Mike

"Oh, my God," I said, looking at the bracelet. It was a one carat, diamond, Rolex-style line tennis bracelet set in ten karat white gold.

"Who was it?" Jeremy asked, coming into the living room.

"It was the UPS truck. He dropped off this package," I said, unsnapping the lock on the bracelet.

"Was it that new game I asked you to order?"

"No, I didn't order the game yet."

"Wow, where did you get that?" he asked, admiring the diamonds.

"Mike sent it to me," I said proudly. "Isn't it beautiful? Here, help me fasten it. I want to see how it looks on my arm."

After Jeremy helped me put it on, I admired it for at least an hour. I just could not believe that man. How could I be so lucky? I wasn't taking it off until after I talked to my baby later that night.

♫♪♫♪♫♪♫♪♫

"Hey, baby."

"Hey, girl. How are you doing?"

"Great. You are so amazing."

"Am I? And why is that?"

"I got the package you sent me today and this bracelet is gorgeous."

"So, you like it?"

"Do I like it? What a question? I don't think I'll ever take it off."

"I was looking online a couple of days ago and when I saw it, I knew my baby had to have it. I got you something else, too. You should get it tomorrow."

"You did? Why thank you, baby, but I don't think anything can top this."

"We'll see. When the other package comes, I want you to wait 'til I call you to open it. It will make me feel like I am there with you. I want to hear the expression in your voice when you open it up."

"Now you got me curious. Will you give me a hint?"

"Nope, you are just going to have to wait and see."

"Ah man, this is torture. Baby, you have no idea how much you mean to me."

"Don't you ever lose that feeling, ok? How is your job coming along?"

"It's ok, things have slowed down some. I thought about buying a house here. It will be good to finally have something of my own. I don't mind living on post, but I like my space."

"If that's what you want, go for it. That's what I love about you, you are a go getter. I hope you find something you like."

"I will. It may take a little time, but I will."

"Ok, babe. Well listen, I got to go. I got a lot of work to catch up on. Remember, when you get the package, don't open it, ok?"

"Ok. Baby, don't you work too hard."

"I won't. I'll talk to you soon."

"Ok, bye."

When I went to bed that night, I was so excited about my day and the gift that would be coming the next day, I couldn't sleep. I knew I had to thank the man who was responsible for all of this. "Dear Heavenly Father, please forgive me for my many sins and thank You for waking me up this morning and for bringing me from a mighty long way. Thank You for Your numerous blessings and for bringing Mike into my life. Every day is worth living because of him and he has made me so happy. Thank You for guiding my footsteps and leading me straight to him, good looking out. Please, protect him and my children from all harm and danger. Thank You for my health, my family, and for my job. None of this would be possible without You. I pray for all mankind, including those who have hurt me. I forgive them like You forgive me. Please, continue to bless us, Dear Lord, Amen."

♫♪♫♪♫♪♫♪

I woke up bright and early the next day. I got Jeremy up and he got ready for school while I made breakfast. "Come on, Jeremy, you're going to be late!" I yelled.

"I'm coming, I'm coming," he said, sounding half asleep.

"Did you go to bed when I told you to?"

"Yes, ma'am, but I am still tired."

"Eat your oatmeal, it's almost time for the bus."

"Why are you in such a good mood this morning?" he asked.

"Aren't I always in a good mood?"

"Not this early in the morning. You're usually grumpy."

He was right. I was definitely not a morning person, but after the bracelet I got yesterday and the gift I knew was coming, I had every right to be in a good mood.

"I'm just happy to be here sharing breakfast with the man of the house."

"If you say so, but we eat breakfast together every morning and you've never been in this good a mood."

"I am expecting another package today so when you get home and there's a box at the door, put it in my room, ok? And, don't open it."

"Un huh. I knew there was a catch. How many gifts is he going to send you?"

"I don't know, but I hope he doesn't stop."

"He's spoiling you."

"I know, and I like it."

Jeremy got on the bus and I left for work. It didn't take me long to get there since I lived on post. "Good morning, Deborah," I said as I walked by her desk.

"Good morning," she replied with a puzzled look on her face. I hardly ever spoke to anyone when I came in but that morning was different. I turned on my computer and could hardly work because I was so excited about my new bracelet and the secret gift I was getting later on. "What in the world is wrong with you?" she asked as she came and stood by my door.

"Look at this, girl," I said, going into my bag to pull out my bracelet.

"Sara, this is beautiful. Where did you get it?"

"Mike sent it to me yesterday. Now do you see why I'm so happy? And, he told me to expect another box today," I said, beginning to cry.

"Why in the world are you crying?"

"Because I am so happy. I am not used to anybody giving me anything. I hit the jackpot when I met him. I wish he was here with me right now."

"You better hold on to him. It ain't too many of him around."

"I know, and there ain't no way I'm letting my Mexican baby go."

"I don't blame you. Let me go and pretend I'm working, I'll see you around."

"Alright."

I caught up on most all my work and was about to leave for the day when my boss called me into his office. "Sergeant Thompson, we have another trip coming up in a few weeks that I would like for you to go on. You are the subject matter expert for what we are promoting and I really need you on this one."

"How long will this trip be?"

"About three days. I hope it is not a problem." Of course, it was a problem, it was always a problem.

"I'll see what I can do, sir."

"Thanks."

"Not a problem." Any other day, I would have been pissed the heck off, but not that day. Nobody was going to kill my joy today. "Hey, Jeremy, is everything ok?" I asked, calling him from the car.

"Yes, ma'am."

"Are you doing your homework?"

"We didn't have any." That boy hated to do his homework.

"I'll just get on the Internet when I get home and see."

"I have a little."

"Well, you better get started, and I'm going to check it when you get done. I am on my way home."

"Ain't you going to ask about your box?"

"Did it come?"

"Yes, I put it on your bed."

"Alright, thank you. I'll see you in a few."

"Bye."

♫♪♫♪♫♪♫♪♫

I got home, took a shower, and tried to relax while I waited for Mike to call. It was still early, so I knew it would still be a few hours before I heard from him. I checked Jeremy's homework, cooked, and laid down across the bed, wishing time away. I couldn't imagine what would be better than the bracelet I had already gotten. I would just have to wait and see, but the anticipation was killing me. I almost drifted off to sleep when the phone rang.

"Hello?"

"Hey, Mom. How are you doing?"

"Hey, Jaylen, I'm doing fine. How are you?"

"I'm doing ok. I didn't get the assignment I wanted to Japan. Instead, I'm going to NS Norfolk, Va."

"That's right down the road from me. You don't want to come to Virginia?"

"I do, I just had my hopes up for Japan. At least I'll be close to you."

"When do you have to report?"

"I will be getting my orders tomorrow. I should be there by Monday."

"I'm happy you'll be close by for your first assignment. You don't have to be all up under me, but you know you will always have a place to go."

"I know. Well I just wanted to call and tell you that. I'll try and call again tomorrow."

"Ok, love you!"

"Love you, too."

Ok, it's 8:00. Mike should be calling any minute now. I had the package right by the bed. I didn't want to waste no time opening it up. I was about to go to the bathroom when the phone rang. I knew it was him from the caller ID.

"Hey, baby."

"Hey, beautiful. How are you doing?"

"Better now that I am talking to you. How was your night?"

"Oh it wasn't bad, cold as usual, didn't get much sleep. I have to go out to the warehouse today and do a couple of things. Did you get the package?"

"Yes, I got it."

"Are you ready to open it?"

"Baby, I have been waiting for you to call all day."

"Ok then, go ahead and open it."

"I am going to put you on speaker phone, ok?"

"Ok."

I put the phone on the night stand and opened the package. "I feel like a kid at Christmas."

"Well, we can pretend this is Christmas," he said.

I pulled out a small red box that looked like it could have held a pair of earrings or possibly a ring. "Ok, whatever it is, it's in a small red box."

"Keep going," he said. I opened the box and immediately put it on the bed. Inside the box was a pair of three-fourth carat, eighteen-carat gold diamond stud earrings. "Hello, are you there?" he asked after a few seconds of silence.

"I'm here, baby," I answered. "I just don't know what to say."

"How about I love you?"

"What did you say?"

"I said I love you."

"Baby, you have no idea how I've longed to hear those words. I love you, too. I love you so much, but, baby, I am so scared. This is all happening so fast," I said with tears going everywhere.

"Do you want me to slow down?"

"No! Please don't slow down. I wish you were here right now so you could make love to me and to put these earrings in my ears."

"Put them on and take a picture with both the earrings and the bracelet and send them to me. I can't wait to see how they look on my baby."

"Baby, I don't know what happened between you and your ex and I don't wanna know. I am so glad you are mines now and I definitely ain't going to let you go."

"Baby, I told you I wasn't going anywhere. I am yours for life, that's if you'll have me that long."

"As long as you stay the way you are, we will always be together."

"That's what I want to hear. Now, dry those tears. If I was there, I'd kiss them dry."

"Can you get a web cam over there?"

"Yeah, they have them at the Post Exchange."

"As soon as I get my own computer, I am going to get one. I would love to see your handsome face while we're talking."

"That's a great idea. We might be able to do some other things, too."

"Your wish is my command."

"Is that right? So you don't mind getting a little kinky every now and then?"

"What I want is to keep my baby happy."

"Ok, well you know what time it is, babe. Duty calls."

"I know. I hate it when you have to go.

"You say that now, but when I get there, you'll probably be glad to throw me out."

"Never."

"Ok, babe, I'll call you again tomorrow. Don't forget to send me some pictures, alright?"

"I won't."

"Love you, baby."

"I love you, too."

"Bye."

It was always hard hanging up the phone after talking to him and now that I knew that he loved me, I was going to do everything in my power to make him happy. I went over to the mirror and started unscrewing the back off the earrings so that I could try them on. They didn't look that big in the box, but they were huge in my ear. I hardly ever wore jewelry, but now that my baby was upgrading me, I was definitely going to start. All I needed was to buy a house. It was definitely time for me to have my own place.

Chapter 35

The next day, I contacted a realtor and told her what I was looking for and the price range I'd like to stay in. There were several houses on the market that she thought I'd be interested in, so I made an appointment for later that day. When I arrived at her office, she was getting ready to walk out the door.

"Gloria?" I asked.

"Yes, hi, you must be Sara. I was just on my way out to meet you. How do you do?" she asked, extending her hand.

"Doing great," I said, shaking it.

"Good! I've mapped out a few areas I thought you'd be interested in. Are you ready to take a look?"

"Let's go," I said, getting into her Mercedes.

We had gone to several houses before we went to a new housing development. "I think you would like it here. As you can see, there is new construction going up every day, and you can pretty much have your house built the way you want it."

"Are any of these within my budget?"

"Yeah, pretty much all of them are and this is a good area because the schools are good and you're close to the base."

"Can we look inside a couple of them?"

"Sure. Let's start with this one." We walked into a house that was partially finished. It had four bedrooms, three bathrooms, and two fireplaces, one in the great room and the other one in the spacious master suite, which also had a sitting area. There was a formal dining room, an eat-in kitchen, a two car garage, and a nice deck area.

"Wow, this is nice!" I said, walking out the back door to the huge back yard.

"If you like this one, we can screen in the back porch. We could even put up a privacy fence. You can pick out all the cabinets, the carpets, and did you like the master bath with the two walk in closets?"

"Yes, I love the size of this house. How many square feet is it?"

"Let me see," she said, looking through her papers. "Twenty-eight hundred."

"Are you sure I can afford this?"

"Yes, it's within your budget."

"Man, I feel like the Jeffersons, I'm moving on up. When will I be able to move in?"

"It is supposed to be complete in three months."

Good, that would be right around the time my baby comes home. "Ok, I think this one is it. I am not going to give you a final answer until I go home and think about it though, but I really do like it. I like everything about it."

"Well, good. You just give me a call when you're ready, but right now is the best time to buy. The rates are really good right now."

"Ok, I'll give you a call tomorrow." It was late when I got in and I was glad there were leftovers in the fridge because I definitely didn't feel like cooking. "Hey, sweetie," I said, peeping my head into Jeremy's room.

"Hey," he said, gazing at me briefly as he played his game.

"Did you do homework?"

"Yes, ma'am."

"Ok, I'm going to take a shower and turn in. You know what time to go to bed."

"Yes, ma'am."

"Alright." I went in my room, took a shower, and lay across the bed skimming through an *O* magazine when the phone rang. "Hey, baby!" I said.

"Hey to you. How is my favorite girl?"

"Doing good, just a little tired."

"I can tell. It don't sound like you are glad to hear from me."

"Baby, I live for your phone calls, don't even go there. How was your night?"

"I slept pretty good, I dreamed about you."

"Oh yeah, I hope it was a good dream."

"It was an excellent dream, I was there with you."

"I sure hope these next few months go by fast 'cause I sure do miss you."

"I miss you, too, you have no idea how much."

"I looked at some houses today and I think I found one."

"You did?"

"Baby, it is so big. It has four bedrooms and the master suite has a fireplace in it. I wish you were here to see it."

"If you like it, go for it. You've always said you wanted your own place, but you know that means you're going to be there for a while."

"I know. I think I can handle it."

"That's good, baby. You go on wit' 'cho bad self."

"You sound so funny saying that," I laughed.

"I do?"

"Yeah, you do."

"Babe?"

"Huh?" I answered.

"You still love me?"

"With all my heart. Did you like the pictures I sent you?"

"Girl, I can't get enough of you."

"I love to hear you say that. Did you get a web cam yet?"

"Uh huh. I picked one up yesterday. When are you going to get the computer?"

"Hopefully, tomorrow. If so, we can use the cameras tomorrow night when you call."

"I can't wait to see my beautiful brown chica."

"I can't wait to see you, either. I love you."

"I love you, too, but, babe?"

"I know, you gotta go."

"Yeah, it's that time."

"I know. You take care, baby, and I'll talk to you soon."

"Ok."

"Remember, I am always thinking about you."

"I am always thinking about you, too. Take care."

"Bye, baby."

"Bye."

The next day, I called Gloria and told her I wanted the house. I made an offer and waited for an answer. I was working on a proposal when she called me with the news. "Hello."

"Hello. Congratulations! It's your house, girl!"

"Yes! Thank You, Jesus!"

"Thank Him, because you will soon be a home owner. I am so happy for you."

"I am happy for me, too. I can't believe it. I think I am going to have to take the rest of the day off."

"You ought to, you deserve it. I am going to start getting the paperwork ready and once everything is finalized and signed, I will hand you the keys to your new house."

"Thank you so much, Gloria. You got me exactly what I wanted."

"You were easy to work for, thank you. I'll be in touch."

I did take the rest of the day off. I was too happy to work. It was a major accomplishment for me. *God, You have really brought me from a mighty long way. Thank You.*

"Hello?"

"Angela, I got the house!"

"Good for you! I am so happy for you. Take some pictures of it and put them in a scrapbook. It's not every day somebody moves into a brand new house. I can't wait to see it."

"It really ain't too much to see yet. They still have a couple of months before they're finished. It might get a bit overwhelming picking out everything."

"At least you get a chance to personalize it. You'll do well. You need to celebrate now."

"I am. I am going to drink a margarita and Jeremy is going to drink a ginger ale," I said, laughing.

"If you need any help, give me a call. I'll be there."

"Bet. Talk to you later." I was so happy, I called everybody I knew. I could not believe it. Life was so funny; you never know where it was going to lead you. I was so glad I didn't give up. Look at all the blessings I would have missed.

♫♪♫♪♫♪♫♫

"Mama, you never cease to amaze me. You are my hero and I am so glad you are my mama," Shanna said, returning my phone call.

"Thank you, sweetie, I am glad you feel that way. The older I get, the more I realize that if you believe in yourself, the possibilities are endless."

"You have everything you ever wanted; a good job, a wonderful man, you're driving a Lexus GX 470, you got money in the bank, and now you got a brand new house. You did it all by yourself. I'm speechless. You are a phenomenal woman."

"Don't forget about you guys. Ya'll are worth more than all of this stuff put together. Ya'll are my reasons for not giving up. Maybe it took me going through all I went through to really appreciate where I am. I truly know what it means to struggle and no matter how painful it was, as you can see, there's a blessing in the storm."

"If I was there right now, I'd give you a hug."

"You have always been a good girl, Shanna, and believe it or not, I drew my strength from you. All those times I wanted to give up, I looked at you. I knew you deserved a decent life and it was my responsibility to give you my best, and look at you today. I am proud of you."

"It was all because of you, lady, it was all because of you. I gotta go, but I'll call you in the morning. Congratulations again!"

"Thank you, talk to you soon."

I was definitely in the mood to celebrate. I went to the Class Six and got some tequila and margarita mix for me and some ginger ale for Jeremy. I then went to pick up the computer so that I could start talking to my baby live. It was good we had email, better when we talked on the phone, but the web cam had to be the next best thing to being together.

"Hey, Mom," Jeremy said when I walked into the house.

"Hey!" I said excitedly.

"I have a couple of bags in the truck, will you go get them for me?"

"Yes, ma'am," he said, walking toward the door. When he came back in, I proudly told him the good news.

"Jeremy, we got the house," I said, walking into the kitchen where he was putting the bags away.

"You did?"

"Yep. I'll take you by there to see it tomorrow."

"Sweet! Will I still be going to the same school?"

"Yes, you sure will. The house is just down the road from here."

"When are we moving?"

"In a couple of months. Do you feel like having a celebration drink with me?"

"Uh huh, what are we drinking?"

"Me, a margarita, and you a ginger ale."

"A ginger ale, that's all I get?"

"Yep, when you turn twenty-one, we'll have another celebration drink," I said, smiling.

"Ok, let's have our drink. I am glad we're moving into our own place. Thanks."

"Me too," I said, fixing our drinks. "To our new house!" I said, holding up my glass.

"To our new house," Jeremy echoed.

We drank our drinks, talked a while, and headed to our rooms. I took the computer upstairs and started hooking everything up. After I got everything together, I hooked up the camera and hoped it all worked. When I saw myself on the computer screen, I knew everything was ready. I was ready for my baby when he called. I couldn't wait to see his face again.

Chapter 36

"Hey, baby!" I said, answering the phone later that night.

"Well hello, beautiful. How are you today?"

"Great, baby, just great."

"You sure sound a lot better than yesterday. What happened?"

"I got the house!" I said excitedly.

"You did? Baby, that is great."

"I know. I am so excited."

"You should be. That's the American dream. I am so happy for you."

"Thanks, baby. I got the computer and web cam today. Can you hook up?"

"Ah yeah, I think so. Let's try it out."

I turned the computer on, turned on the camera, and waited. "Baby, it's asking you for permission."

"Ok, I gave you permission, now you have to give me permission."

"Ok. Can you see me?"

"Yes, I see my beautiful chica. You are so cute."

"I can't see you yet. Ok, there you are. Hey, baby."

"Hey," he said, waving.

"Baby, you look so good," I said, smiling. "I can't wait 'til you get home."

"I can't wait to get there, either. You are so beautiful."

"You make me feel beautiful, inside and out. Who was that that just walked by?"

"That was my buddy, Will. He works in the warehouse. He is a pretty good guy. We hang out and play cards sometimes after work."

"Oh, that's good."

"Yes, it helps the time pass until I can come home to my chica."

"Do you still wear the necklace?"

"I sure do," he said, pulling it from under his shirt.

"Me too," I said, showing him mine. "What are you going to do today?"

"Well, I got some paperwork to catch up on and tomorrow, I have to go into Iraq to track some equipment."

"How long will you be gone?"

"I should come back the same day. Don't worry, girl, I'll be ok."

"I am always going to worry about you. Be careful."

"You know I will. I got to get home to my baby."

"That's right."

"Ok, babe, I hate to cut this short, but I got a meeting to go to."

"Ok. I am glad we got these cameras. It was so good seeing your face."

"Me too, gorgeous. I'll try and call before I leave."

"Ok."

"You take care now."

"I will," I said, blowing him a kiss. Bye."

"Bye."

I always worried when he took those trips. They were so dangerous. I knew he was doing what he loved, taking care of the troops, but I loved him too and would be glad when he decided to come back for good. I didn't think I would ever get tired of having him around.

♫♪♫♪♫♪♫♪

I was so glad it was the weekend. Sleeping in felt so good. I drug myself up and went into the kitchen to make me a cup of coffee when the doorbell rang. I got excited when I opened the door and saw Jaylen standing there.

"Good morning," he said, stepping in and giving me a hug.

"Hey, you, what a pleasant surprise. Come on in," I said, leading him into the kitchen. "Have you had breakfast yet?"

"Yeah, I grabbed something on the way out."

"What brings you this way?"

"I was missing ya'll and decided to stop by. Do you have anything planned for the day?"

"Not really. I'm taking Jeremy by to see the house. I will be moving in soon. They have done so much since I last went by there."

"Well, I came by right on time. I can't wait to see it. I know it's beautiful."

"It is, son, I love it."

"Have you talked to Shanna lately?"

"I talk to her all the time. She said she was bringing Tyler up so that I can meet him. He seems like a nice fella."

"He is, I met him. They get along really well. I just hope he knows what he's getting into."

"Why do you say that?"

"That girl is tough. As long as he don't make her mad, he's ok, because that girl don't play."

"Yeah, she is tough, but she got a heart of gold, you know that."

"Yeah, I'm just glad she's my sister."

"Hey, Jaylen," Jeremy said, walking into the kitchen.

"Hey, knucklehead," Jaylen said, rubbing him upside the head.

"Hey, watch it," Jeremy said irritably.

"Played any new games lately?"

"Naw, Mom took the system away from me. I got a C- on my report card."

"Oh, I remember those days."

"Yeah, tell me about it."

"I'm going to go get dressed. We'll leave in about an hour," I said, walking out of the kitchen.

♫♪♫♪♫♪♫♫

"Ma, you outdid yourself. This house is off the chain. Can I move back home?" he teased once we got to the house.

"You can come visit anytime you like."

"This is my room over here," Jeremy said, showing Jaylen his room.

"Man, this junk is tight. You got your own bathroom. Ya'll living the life. It's so much space in here, are you going to be able to fill it all up?"

"Not all at once, but eventually."

"I am going to love bringing my lady over here."

"Oh, there is a lady in your life now?" I asked.

"I got a little something, something going on, nothing serious."

"Uh huh, you go, boy." We left the house, and went out to the mall and did some shopping before going back home.

"Mom, there is another package at the door," Jeremy said as we pulled into the driveway.

"Man, what did you do to this guy?" Jaylen asked.

"Just loved him, that's all."

"She has gotten a lot of packages from him. He sends her diamonds, pearls, everything. He got her spoiled," Jeremy continued.

"She deserves to be spoiled," Jaylen said, giving me a kiss on the cheek.

We went in and watched a movie before Jaylen decided it was time for him to go back to his room. "It was cool hanging out with ya'll today, but I got this mad date tonight. I'll be back by in a couple of weeks."

"Ok, Jaylen, thanks for stopping by. You treat that girl right now."

"I will. Jeremy, bring those grades up so we can play a game when I come back."

"Yeah, yeah," Jeremy replied. We all hugged as he walked out the door.

♪♫♪♫♪♫♪♫

Time was really flying. Before I knew it, it was time to move into the house and plenty of people came to help; Angela and Vanessa, JaLisa, Shanna and her fiancé, Tyler, Cheyenne and her new husband, Adrian, and Jaylen. Mama still couldn't make the trip, but promised to make the next one. There was plenty of room for everybody. After we moved everything in and got it situated, we ordered pizza and played dominos, spades, and *Taboo*. Tyler, Adrian, and Jaylen went out and got some drinks and we were up most of the night listening to music, laughing about old times, and just having a great time.

"I wish all the people who talked all that trash about Janet's children could see us now," JaLisa said.

"Ain't that the truth? I bet all those that have passed on are turning over in their graves," Angela added.

"I don't know why they treated us that way, wasn't any of us bad," I said.

"That's what makes it so bad, and all the ones they put up on those pedestals, look at them today. If they ain't on drugs, they drunks, look at Kat. She so strung out, she don't even know who she is most of the time," JaLisa said.

"What? I can't believe that," I said in disbelief.

"Girl, she look so bad, you wouldn't even recognize her, and she was the apple of everybody's eye. God has a way of turning things around. The last shall be first, and the first shall be last," JaLisa said.

I felt so bad for Kat. I hated her growing up, having to live in her shadow, but when I got older, I realized it wasn't her fault they treated us differently. She had so much going for her. I prayed she could break her addiction.

"I wonder what all the ones living would say if they walked through that door right now?" Vanessa said.

"They wouldn't come 'cause they'd be too ashamed," JaLisa said. "But, you can best believe they gon' know when I get back home. I'm going to preach it from the pulpit and don't let me see your boy, Jacob. I can't wait to rub it in his face," she continued.

"I look at us as blessed. I ain't mad at him. He slowed me down, but he didn't stop me."

"Girl, you the bomb. You had it worst of all, but you could never tell it by looking at you today. I don't know how you did it," JaLisa said.

"I couldn't do none of it by myself, it was all by the grace of God."

"Amen to that," Angela said. We all talked until we started passing out one by one. I felt lonely after they all left. I liked the closeness of family. We always stuck together.

I think I did a good job picking out everything. My favorite two rooms were the kitchen and the master suite. The kitchen's theme was black and white. The cabinets were white with black knobs, the walls were painted sage green, and all the appliances were stainless steel with black trim. The counter tops were black granite with little specks of white, the double sinks were white with stainless steel fixtures, and the ceiling fan had black blades with white globes. I loved the bar area which was able to seat six people.

The master suite held my king sized bed, and I had a chaise and recliner in the sitting area which was centered around the fireplace. The master bath had a separate shower with two spa shower heads and one hand held shower, and a six jet Jacuzzi. All of the floors were hardwood except the bathrooms and kitchen, which were gray marble. The outside of the house was made of red brick with four white columns on the front porch and the trim around the windows and door was also white. It had a big front yard and I did have the back porch screened in, and I could enter it from my bedroom. Another one of my favorite features was that the house was on a cul-de-sac, which meant little traffic. I loved everything about it. *Better Homes and Garden* didn't have nothing on me.

Chapter 37

"Hey, baby," I said happily when Mike called that night.

"Hey, girl, you feeling better?"

"Yeah. I don't know why I let things get to me, but I am doing much better now that I am talking to you." I had had a bad day at work and vented to him the last time he called.

"Well, I'm glad. Are you getting settled into your new house?"

"Uh huh, I can't wait for you to see it."

"I can't wait, either. I know it is as beautiful as you are. I can't wait for us to get into the Jacuzzi."

"Me neither, baby."

"You know what, girl?"

"What?"

"I am so proud of you, do you know that? You are so strong and independent. You have accomplished so much and you did it all by yourself. I like the way you go after things and make them happen. That is one of the qualities that attracted me to you and in just a few short weeks, we'll be together again. I am about to start counting down the days."

"Start? I started counting down a long time ago. I can't wait to get you here. Do you have time to get on the web cam?"

"I got a few minutes, I'll hook it up."

"Ok. I hope we get a good connection this time. Can you see me?"

"Not yet, wait a minute. Ok, now I see my beautiful brown chica," he said with a big ole grin. "What's that on your head?"

"You know that's my scarf, baby. Don't play."

"I know, baby, I was just messing with you. You know I like your scarves."

"Do you like this?" I asked, lifting up my shirt.

"Wooo, do I? Don't you start nothing. Do that again," he said, getting closer to the camera.

"What, this?" I asked, lifting my shirt again, shaking my girls like I was in a strip club.

"Baby, baby, baby, I'm on my way home right now."

"Well come on then, big boy. I'm here waiting for you," I said, slipping down my pants, exposing my sweet potato pie.

"Aw, girl, you are making me so hot."

"Am I?" I asked, taking a finger and inserting it inside me.

"Baby, you got to stop. You are getting me so aroused."

"Are you, baby? You want some of this sweet potato pie?"

"Can I eat the whole thing?"

"You can have it all. Ut oh, baby, I think I lost you. Can you still see me?"

"No, baby, the system went down again. Dammit. Girl, you got my Johnson so hard."

"You go take a cold shower. I don't want you giving my sweetness to nobody but me."

"You are going to be in trouble when I get there."

"Why, baby? Am I being a naughty girl?"

"Yeah. I'm going to have to give you a spanking."

"Umm, I got something to look forward to then."

"Yes, you do. Well, listen, girl, I got to go. You know I'm going to be thinking about you all day. Remember I have to go back into Iraq and track the rest of that equipment, and hopefully, I'll be back later on today. If not, I'll give you a call as soon as I get back."

"Be safe, baby."

"I'll be fine, girl, no worries. I'll call you when I can, ok?"

"Ok, I love you."

"I love you, too, bye."

♫♪♫♫♪♫♪♫

"Hey, Ma, how are you?" Shanna asked when I answered the phone later that night.

"I'm doing good, still trying to get this house together. What are you up to?"

"Nothing much. I thought about coming for a visit but I got to hurry up, don't I? Your man will be coming in soon, won't he?"

"Yes, he'll be here in a couple of weeks."

"Don't you mess around and have no babies now," she said, teasing.

"I don't know. I've been thinking about it."

"Are you serious?"

"No, but if I had met him ten years ago, I'd give him all the babies he wanted, but I think I am a little too old to be thinking about having more kids."

"Mom, people are having babies in their fifties. You're not even close."

"I'm close enough. I want to be able to take care of them, not have them take care of me."

"Do you have anything special planned for you and Mike?"

"If you weren't my daughter, I'd tell you."

"Ooh, I'm going to tell Jaylen," she said, laughing.

"Didn't ya'll say it was about time? It is, and I am going to enjoy every minute of it."

"I ain't mad at you and if you do get pregnant, I'll help you take care of it."

"Whatever! When are you planning on coming?"

"The weekend. I feel like hanging out with you since Tyler will be going out of town."

"Have ya'll set a date yet?"

"We thought about next spring, but we're not sure yet."

"Whenever ya'll decide, you know I'll help you in any way I can."

"I know, thanks. Ok, I just wanted to holla. I'll call you before I come."

"Ok, talk to you later."

♫♪♫♪♫♪♫♪

It had been several days since I heard from Mike and I was beginning to get worried. I knew he had done this plenty of times before and he had always made it back safely. I would give anything to hear his voice right then.

"Good morning, Sergeant Thompson," Deborah said when I went to work the next morning.

"Hey," I said, walking straight to my desk. I put my bags down and was about to turn on my computer when I looked up and saw her standing there.

"Wake up on the wrong side of the bed this morning?"

"What do you think?" I asked, not caring that I was being rude, but I wasn't in the mood for talking.

"Well, if you want to talk about it, I'll be at my desk," she said, walking away.

"Wait a minute, Deb. I'm sorry. I'm just on edge. Mike left to go on a mission and I haven't heard from him in a few days, and I am so worried about him."

"Hasn't he done this before?"

"Yes, but it's getting so close to time for him to come home, I'm just a little scared. I pray nothing happens to him."

"He'll be fine. I don't know how you do it, though. If it was my man over there, I don't think I could handle it. I'd be a basket case."

"It is hard being separated, but love conquers all. If you really, truly love each other, nothing should tear you apart. Anything worth having is worth fighting for. Who said love is painless? Mike and I have a great relationship and we talk every day. I never knew love like this before him, and I like it. There are so many families separated right now because of the war, and there's no end in sight. We're losing soldiers every day. I don't want my man to leave me because I made a vow to serve my country which may cause me to deploy at any time, and that's why I'm standing by Mike, but is it wrong for me to miss him so much?"

"No, that's what true love does to you. Keep your head up. I'm sure you will hear from him soon."

"I hope so. I guess I need to get some work done, maybe that will keep my mind off of him."

"I'll be at my desk if you need me," she said, rubbing me on my shoulder.

"Thanks," I said as she was walking out of my office.

I went to get some coffee while I waited for the computer to install all its updates. When I got back in and logged on, the notifier informed me that I had three new messages. *Please, let Mike be one of them.* I prayed. *Thank You, Jesus!*

Babe,

I am doing fine, so stop worrying. I am stuck here and am waiting for a flight back. If I don't get out tonight, I will take a convoy back tomorrow which will probably take all day. As soon as I get in, I will give you a call. I miss you and will see you next week. I love you, girl. Talk to you soon.

Mike

Thank you Lord. Whew, I felt so much better. I was so glad it was my last week working, my nerves were shot. I needed this time to get the house perfect and get ready for my baby.

"Let's hang that picture over here," Shanna said as we were doing some last minute touches on the house.

"Yeah, that looks good," I said, admiring the room. "Let's take a break, we have been at it all day. My back hurts."

"Wait 'til Mike gets done with you if you think your back hurts now," Shanna said, grinning.

"I'm looking so forward to that. I'll call you to come help me get out of bed," I said proudly.

"What day is he coming in?"

"He made reservations for next Friday, but this has been a bad week."

"What happened?"

"He had to go on a mission and now he is stuck trying to get back. He was trying to get a flight and if that didn't work, he was going to take a convoy. I haven't heard from him since Tuesday, but I am not going to worry. I have to believe that he is ok."

"He is. If he is convoying, it may take him a couple of days. They have so many check points now, so what used to take two days sometimes turn out to be a week. He'll call when he gets in, don't worry." We were in the kitchen putting away dishes when the doorbell rang. "Do you want me to get that?" Shanna asked.

"No, I'll get it," I said, making my way to the door. When I opened the door, I didn't recognize the two gentlemen who were standing there. "May I help you?" I asked, thinking they had the wrong address.

"Ma'am, my name is William and this is Vance, and we are looking for Sara Johnson," a tall, white gentleman asked.

"May I ask what for?" I asked curiously.

"We have a letter to give her, special delivery."

"Who is it, Mom?" Shanna asked, coming to the door.

"I am Sara, you can give the letter to me," I said nervously.

"Ma'am, I am sorry to tell you this, but Mike was involved in an accident and..."

"Mom, get up, Mom!" I heard Shanna scream as she was slapping me in the face.

After I snapped out of it, I immediately looked up to see if the two men were still there or wondering if I was having a bad dream. When I looked up and saw them, I started screaming, "Nooooo! This is not happening to me! No, no no no!" as I tried to get up, but each time I tried, my legs would buckle and I'd fall back down.

"Come on, Mom, let me help you," Shanna said, trying to pick me up off the porch.

"Please, Lord, please tell me this is a dream, please, Lord, please! I want my baby, Lord, I want my baby!" I screamed. "This cannot be happening. Mike will be here next week, he'll be here next week," I said babbling, still trying to get up.

"Let me go get you some water," Shanna said, crying.

"I don't want no water, I want Mike!" I screamed.

"Ma'am, please let us help you into the house," Vance said.

"Get away from me! This must be a mistake. Mike said he was fine. It has to be a mistake!"

It felt like Shanna rocked me for hours as I lay crying in her lap. "You ready to go in the house now?" she whispered in my ear.

"I think so," I said, trying to stand up again.

"Here, let me help you," William said, grabbing me by the arm. He grabbed one arm and Shanna grabbed the other one.

"I want to go to my room. I want to lie down," I cried.

"Ok, Mom, we're going to your room."

Halfway there, I started screaming again. "I cannot believe this, I just cannot believe this. Mike, baby, please come back, please come back!" I cried, sinking to the floor.

William picked me up and carried me the rest of the way. Jeremy had just gotten home and was wondering what all the commotion was about. Shanna grabbed him by the hand and took him out of the room.

"Sara, Mike wanted me to give you this letter and this package. We had this system. Every time any one of us went out on mission, we would leave an envelope with one of our buds to give to our loved ones just in case something happened, but we always got it back because we made it back safely every time. This is the first time we actually had to use the system. He got this package the day before he left and gave it to me also. I am going to leave them here on your night stand. I am also leaving you my phone number just in case you have any questions."

"I do have a question," I said struggling to get up. "What happened to Mike?"

"Well, he couldn't get a flight back from Iraq so he opted to take a convoy. He said he was trying to get home to his baby. The convoy was ambushed and his vehicle left the road for a split second and hit an IED. Three people were killed. Mike was one of them. Sara, Mike didn't suffer and he loved you very much. We knew who you were when you answered the door 'cause he had pictures of you everywhere. You are all he talked about and couldn't wait to get back home to you. His body is being shipped to Colorado, and as soon as we find out when he'll be laid to rest, we'll let you know. Is there anything else?"

"Not right now," I said, laying back down.

"Call me if you need me. We'll be here until they hold his funeral."

"Thank you. He was crazy about you guys, too. He spoke of you often," I managed to say.

"Yeah, he was a good man, Mike was," William said, looking like he was reminiscing on some memorable moments. "We are all going to miss him."

Darkness fell quickly, and I laid there and cried softly as I looked at Mike's pictures. We were so happy together. *Why did this have to happen to us?*

"Here, Mom, I brought you some hot tea. I hope it makes you feel a little better. Shanna is making you something to eat," Jeremy said, sitting the tea down on the tray. "I'm sorry, Mom. I wish there was something I could do."

"Just lay here with me," I said. "Lay here and hold my hand." I looked at the clock and realized it was the time Mike usually called and I started crying uncontrollably. Jeremy went out, I guess to get Shanna because they both came back in the room together. "Mike would be calling me any minute now if he was still here," I cried.

"I know, Mom, but you know he is in Heaven waiting for you," Shanna said, rubbing my hair.

"I don't want him in Heaven, I want him here with me!" I cried.

They didn't say anything else for a few minutes. They just let me cry it out. "Mom, when are you going to open the letter and package?" she asked.

"I don't know. I don't have the strength to do it now. It is all too painful."

"It might make you feel better." I didn't say anything. "Well, we'll be downstairs if you need anything. Try to eat something. Ok?" she said, kissing me on the cheek.

"I'll be in my room. Call me if you need something," Jeremy said. "I love you," he said, leaving the room.

"I love you, too," I whispered.

I could not sleep. All I could think about was Mike and all of our broken dreams. *Why is it people can treat you like a dog and they stay around for years, but when you get someone who treats you so well, they only stay for a little while?* Life simply wasn't fair. *I need to read the letter. I don't know when I'll get the strength. I may as well read it and get it over with.* I reached over and grabbed it off the night stand. *Lord, please give me the strength.* I took a deep breath as I began to open it.

My sweet Sara. "I can't do this, Lord, I can't do this!" I cried, putting the letter down. "Pleeease, Lord, help me through this." I picked up the letter and tried reading through my tears.

My sweet Sara, I am so, so sorry. I did not mean to put you through so much pain. I tried my best to make it back to you, but I guess God had a different plan. I loved you more than I loved anyone in my life and I'm glad I had you all the way to the end. There was not one minute that I didn't think about you. You gave me a reason to smile. I had control over a lot of things, but this one was out of my hands. I'm sure when I took my last breath, I was thinking about you. You are so beautiful and such a good person, I know you will eventually find someone who will make you happy again. Don't hold back. Live your life to the fullest and never forget that you were my life and I want you to continue to live. I love you, my beautiful brown chica, and I'll be waiting for you in heaven. Goodbye.

I closed the letter and put it in my drawer. I picked up the package and began to open it as the tears streamed down my face. Inside was a small red box. I held my breath and closed my eyes as I opened it up. When I opened it up and saw the diamond ring, I could not hold it in any longer. "Nooooo, no, no, no, no, nooooooo, no, no, no," I cried. Shanna and Jeremy came running into the room.

"It's ok, Mom," Shanna said, hugging me. "Get it all out."

"Whhyyyy, Shanna, whhyyyy? We were so happy. Why did this have to happen?"

"I don't know, Mom, I just don't know," she said, crying.

"Come here, Jeremy," I cried. I grabbed him and hugged him so hard.

"I am sorry I woke you. I'm ok, you go back to sleep ok?"

"I can sleep in here with you if you want me to."

"I know, baby, but I want you to get a good night sleep. I'll only keep you up if you sleep in here. I will see you in the morning, ok?"

"Are you sure?"

"Yes, I'm sure. Good night."

"Good night," he said and went to his room.

"Well, I'm sleeping in here," Shanna said, getting under the covers. "I see you opened the package," she said, wiping the tears from her eyes. "Can I ask you what was in it?"

"Open it up," I said.

She opened the box and laid her head on my chest. "I am so sorry, Mom. I wish I could take all this pain away. Mike loved the hell out of you. The evidence is right here," she said, lifting up the box.

"It didn't take this ring to prove he loved me. I knew it from day one when he gave me nothing but a smile."

"Here, there is a note inside," she said, reaching in the package.

Baby, I wanted to surprise you when I got home and slip this ring on your finger, but you are going to have to do it for me. I guess there is no point in asking you to marry me now, but if I was there, we'd be getting married next week. I'll always love you.

"Now do you see why this hurts so badly? How can I go on?" I asked, putting the note on my night stand.

"One day at a time and I'll be here to help you along the way," Shanna said, reaching over and kissing my tear stained face. "Try and get some sleep," she said, pulling the covers up on me. "I'll be right here."

I picked up the box and took out the ring. I put it on my finger as tears streamed down my face. "I love you, Mike," I said softly. I cradled his picture in my arms, curled up, and went to sleep.

Chapter 38

"Good morning," Shanna said once I finally woke up.

"What time is it?"

"It's a little past eleven."

"Ugh," I moaned, grabbing my pounding head. "I got to get up," I said, throwing the covers off me.

"Easy now," she said, grabbing me by my arm. "I ran you some bath water."

"Thank you," I said as I made my way to the bathroom. I didn't even look in the mirror for fear of shock because I knew I looked a hot mess, but you know what? I didn't even care. As soon as I looked over at the Jacuzzi, I began to cry again. *Get it together, Sara,* I said as I stepped in.

"I can't wait to get you in the Jacuzzi," I remembered Mike saying as reality began to sink in. My baby was gone. There would be no Jacuzzi baths, no showers, or no sweet potato pie. Everything I had been looking forward to had been taken away.

"Is everything alright in there?" I heard a familiar voice say. Tiffany eased the door open and stuck her head in. "Can I come in?" All I could do was cry. She came over and sat on the stool next to the tub. "Here, let me do that for you," she said, taking the sponge.

"When did you get here?" I asked, trying to control my tears.

"About an hour ago. Shanna called me last night and I left out early this morning. Cheryl said she'd be here in a couple of days. She and your mother called while you were still asleep. They told me to tell you that they loved you."

"Tiff, everything was going so good. He was the kindest man I had ever met and the first man to ever tell me he loved me. I keep going over it in my mind and I just don't understand why."

"I wish I knew the answers, but I don't," she said, washing my back. "What I do know is that he loved you very much and that love is what is going to get you through this."

"I don't think I can. This is the hardest thing I've ever had to endure."

"Think about all the joy he brought to your life, don't that make you smile?"

"No, the only thing that will make me smile is if Mike walked through that door," I said, pointing to the door. "Look at this," I said, holding up my hand.

"Sara, that is beautiful," she said, holding my finger. "Didn't I tell you he was going to ask you to marry him?"

"Well, he didn't."

"He would have if he... never mind. When is the last time you ate?"

"I don't know, late yesterday afternoon."

"Well, we need to get you something to eat. Come on, let's go get you something. Shanna has already cooked and I brought some food with me."

"You go ahead, I'll be down in a minute."

"Ok, but if you're not down in fifteen minutes, I'm coming to get you," she said, smiling. "Here, give me a hug," she said, bending over the tub.

I reached up and hugged her ever so tightly. I didn't want to let her go. "Look at you. You are all wet now," I said as she stood up.

"That's ok, I'll dry," she said, wiping away tears. "I'll see you in a few," she said as she walked out the door.

The rest of the day felt like a blur. I remember talking to Jaylen, but only remember parts of the conversation. I knew he said he was coming home, but I persuaded him not to. There was no point. There was nothing anybody could do. I did manage to eat something, but all I wanted to do was lie down and look at Mike's picture. My head hurt something fierce.

"Ma, Aunt Angela is on the phone, do you feel like talking?" Jeremy asked, peeping into the room. Tiffany was sitting in a chair reading and Shanna was lying across the foot of the bed looking at a magazine.

"I'll talk for a few minutes," I said as he brought the phone to me giving me a kiss at the same time. "Thank you," I said, taking the phone. I really didn't feel like talking. "Hello?"

"Hey. How are you feeling?"

"Like shit."

"I bet. I am so sorry, Sara."

"Me too."

"Me and Vanessa are thinking about coming up there."

"No, you don't have to that. I will get through this. Shanna is here and Tiff flew up for a few days. I think I'll be ok."

"Are you sure? We can be there tomorrow?"

"I'm sure. You guys are the best, but I'm going to be ok."

"Well, we'll be thinking about you. Call us if you need us."

"I will."

"Love you, girl."

"Love you, too."

♫♪♫♪♫♪♫♪

It was late the next day when I got a phone call from William. He said the funeral would be held on Friday, the day Mike was supposed to come home. He gave me all the details and said he'd fly me there and put me up in a hotel if I decided to attend.

"Well, are you going?" Tiffany asked, sitting down next to me.

"I don't know. I don't think I can handle seeing him being buried on the same day he was supposed to come back to me. That will be torture. I want to remember him the way he was, not in a casket."

"It will give you a chance to say goodbye," Shanna said, painting my toes.

"I didn't think about it that way. I don't know. I need some time to process this."

"I'll go with you if you want me to," Tiffany suggested.

"Me too," Shanna copied.

"You guys have already done enough. That's probably going to be an expensive ticket with it being such short notice."

"You let me worry about that, ok?" Tiff said.

"Shanna, you're going to fail this semester if you miss too many days," I warned her.

"I already called the school and told them I had a death in the family. They are going to let me make up what I missed."

Family. I sure wished we had become one. "What about Jeremy? He still has school. I can't go."

"When Deborah called the other day, she said she'd be glad to keep Jeremy if you needed her to," Shanna reminded me.

"Just think about it. No pressure. You do what you feel is best for you," Tiff said.

"Hey, Cheryl," I said, looking at the caller ID.

"Hey, I'm at the airport. My flight gets in tonight at 8:30." I forgot all about her coming in.

"Cheryl, you might want to reconsider. Mike's funeral is on Friday and I am debating on whether or not I am going. If I do decide to go, I will be leaving out day after tomorrow."

"Oh, when will you be coming back?"

"Saturday morning."

"I can change my reservations and meet you there if you want me to."

"But, you're already at the airport."

"Yeah, but I really want to see you, Sara. This is the only chance I got. Kenny just got out of the field and will be going back on Monday. If it wasn't for that, I would have been there already."

"I know. Look, come on. I'll figure something out."

Once Cheryl got there and got settled in, we discussed the trip to Colorado. "I called Kenny and told him about the possibility of me going to Colorado. He said it wouldn't be a problem. So, if you decide to go and you want me to go with you, I can. If you need me to stay here and keep Jeremy for you, I can do that, too. I am here for you," she said.

"Thank you." I said giving her a hug. "I still don't know yet."

I left them in the living room and went to my room to decide whether or not I would take the trip. I loved Mike so much, and going to his funeral would be unbearable. *Sara, you are so strong,* I remember him saying.

"No I'm not, baby. Right now I am so weak. It hurts so much," I said, trying not to cry again.

After debating back and forth on what I should do, I decided that I did need to tell my baby goodbye. I think I needed that closure to help me move on. It was the hardest thing I ever had to do, but I had to do it. I had to get it over with. I went down and told them that I had decided to go. Not because I wanted to, but because I needed to. I called William back and told him I'd like to come and that I would need accommodations for four in the hotel. He was so generous; he paid for all of our airfare and the hotel room, and agreed to pick us up at the airport.

"It's time to go, Mom," Shanna said, coming into the room.

"I know. It's just too hard for me to walk out that door. Tomorrow was supposed to be the happiest day of my life, but instead, it will be the saddest."

"We don't have to go if you don't want to."

"I know, but it won't change the fact that he won't be coming home. I guess in a way, going is something to look forward to."

"Oh yeah, why is that?"

"At least tomorrow, we will still be together," I cried.

William and Vance met us at the airport and offered to buy us a rental, which we accepted. They took us to the hotel and told me he'd be back to pick us up at 10:00 on Friday. Mike's service would be at 11:00.

We had some food sent up to the room because I really didn't feel like going out. We made small talk, but my nerves were getting the best of me. I stayed in the bathroom all night. I got up before everyone else the next morning and kneeled down on my knees to pray.

"Dear Lord, please forgive me for my sins, and thank You for all your many blessings. Lord, I know You don't make no mistakes, but I don't understand why this had to happen. I have tried to live a good life, but it seems like bad things always seem to happen to me. Sometimes, I wonder why I'm even here. My life has been one heart break after another, with this being the worst. Please, help me get through the service and thank You for allowing me to love and to be loved. I ask this in Your Holy name. Amen."

By the time I got out of the shower everyone else was up. "Good morning," I said solemnly as I walked out of the bathroom.

"Good morning," they all said somberly. I could not believe that for months I had been looking so forward to this day, but now I was dreading it. By the time we all had our showers and got dressed, it was time for William to come pick us up. I ate very little because my appetite was completely gone.

Mike was having an outdoor service and when we pulled up, his casket was already there. It was draped with the American flag and a band was sitting nearby. There was a big portrait of him on display and immediately my eyes started to water. When I stepped out of the car, the chill in the air made me feel good about my decision to bring a jacket.

"Look at all the flowers," Tiff said as we were exiting the car. I couldn't say anything, I was too numb.

"Are you ready?" Shanna asked.

"I'm ready," I said.

As we walked toward the seats, my legs started to buckle and Shanna and Cheryl had to grab me. They held me all the way to the seat I chose, which was near the back. I could not take my eyes off his picture. He looked so happy in it. "Why did you have to leave me?" I asked softly, still gazing at his picture.

We were there about fifteen minutes when the funeral cars started lining up. I didn't know anybody there so I kept my seat in the back. I recognized his two children because they looked just like him. As soon as they all got seated, the service began.

The service was beautiful. Everything the preacher said about Mike was true. He was a great man and God needed him now. After the preacher prayed his final prayer, I cried softly as we stood while the band played Taps. After the band finished playing, the service ended and people started to leave. I sat back down and stared at Mike's picture and all the beautiful flowers. William and Vance were mingling with the family.

"Are you ok?" Shanna asked, wiping away tears. I shook my head yes. Tiff and Cheryl came over, gave me a big hug, and held my hand. As I remained sitting, William and an older Hispanic woman came down the aisle toward us and she was carrying a box.

"Hi, Sara," she said, extending her frail hand when she got to my seat. I stood up and shook her hand wondering how she knew my name. I guess William must have told her. She was a beautiful woman, not too tall, and wore a beautiful smile on her face resembling Mike's.

"Hi," I responded, releasing her hand.

"I'm Mike's mother and I wanted to speak to you before you left. I wanted to say thank you for making my son so happy. I know it pains you knowing that this was the day he was supposed to come home, and he is home. I know it's not the way we want him home, but he's home. Mike died doing what he loved and that gives me comfort. All of his belongings were sent home and I wanted to give this to you," she said, handing me the box. "I'm sure Mike would want you to have them. If you like, you are welcome to come by the house. We'd be glad to have you."

"Thank you for the invitation, but we have to head back. You are too kind, I see where Mike gets it from. He was the most incredible man I ever met. You must be proud."

"I am. You have no idea how proud I am. Well, I got to go. Everyone is waiting on me. If you do decide to come by, you are welcome. If not, you take care of yourself and thank you again," she said, giving me a hug.

"Thank you for having such a wonderful son," I said, hugging her back.

I sat back down and looked through the box. The first thing I saw was the necklace with the broken heart. I took it out and squeezed it to me. I continued to look through the box to find all the pictures I had ever sent him. It made me smile thinking about how much fun it was taking them for him.

We were the only ones left when her car pulled off. "Will you guys give me a minute?" I asked, handing Cheryl the box.

"Sure take your time," William said.

I walked up the aisle toward the casket. The closer I got, the heavier my legs felt. When I finally got there, I stopped in front of his picture first. When I looked at him, he looked right back at me with a big ole smile on his face. I stroked it and mumbled, "I love you." I went to the casket and laid my head where I thought his chest would be.

"I'm glad you're home, baby. You came just like you said you would. You don't know how badly I wish I could hear you laugh, to see your smile, or to hold you in my arms. I'll love you forever, baby. You're the best and you made me so happy. I'll never forget you. Sleep tight, my love. I'll see you again in Heaven. Goodbye."

I took the necklace and placed it among all the roses that were placed on his casket. As I turned to walk away, I felt a sense of peace. The pain was still there, but my spirit was at peace. Being there was the closure I needed to start healing and to move forward. I wasn't with him that day the way I wanted to be, but I still got to be with my baby.

One Year Later

"Family and friends, I give you Mr. and Mrs. Tyler Daniels!" the preacher said as Shanna and Tyler turned to leave the altar. She looked so radiant in her white, strapless, satin gown that accentuated her slender waistline. It had embroidery, pearl, and crystal beading and sequins and a semi-cathedral train. Her hair was worn in an up-do with a white, beaded, pearl headband. She winked at me as she walked past my pew and I blew her a kiss. I knew she was ready to take life head-on and my prayer for her was that she'd never be mistreated and to try and achieve every goal she set for herself. Through all of our ups and downs, I was glad Jacob was there to give her away. He brought his mama and his girlfriend, too, but that was quite alright with me. He had aged so much over the years and if you didn't know him, you would have thought he was her grandpa instead of her father, but he was still a good looking man, nonetheless. He didn't play too big of a role in their lives growing up, but at least he did come through for her when it really counted.

"How are you doing, Sara?" he asked as I walked out to the waiting limo.

"Doing great, and you?"

"Doing just fine."

"Well, I'm glad. I'm also glad you were here for Shanna. I know it meant a lot to her."

"That's my baby girl. I am glad she thought enough of me to ask."

"You are her daddy, Jacob, nothing will ever change that."

"I know, but I haven't been there like I should have been and I'm sorry."

"I'm sure she'd love to hear you say that," I said.

"I did tell her, right before we walked down the aisle, and I am also sorry for how I treated you. I didn't have the best example to learn from growing up and I simply didn't know any better. I hope you can forgive me."

"I did forgive you, Jacob, a long time ago."

"Come on, Sara. Shanna is about to throw the bouquet!" Vanessa said excitedly.

"Ok, I'm coming," I said, walking in the direction of all the waiting girls.

"Are you staying for the reception?" I asked Jacob.

"Only for a little while. I have to be heading back shortly."

"Ok, I'll see you there," I said as I walked away. I had only taken a few steps when I was stopped again. That time it was by Aunt Wilma. "Well hello, Aunt Wilma. I didn't know you were here," I said, surprised. I hadn't seen her in years.

"Hey, baby, it's so good to see you," she said, reaching out to hug me. Of course, I hugged her back. When we broke our embrace, she looked at me with such admiration. "You've grown into such a beautiful woman. You've raised three beautiful children and have accomplished so much. I am so proud of you," she said with sincerity.

"Thank you, but you know what, Aunt Wilma? I took all the negative things I had ever been told and turned them into something positive. It wasn't easy, but it made me a better person. I used to be ashamed of who I was and of the color of my skin, but not today. I am a beautiful brown sugar and am truly happy to be one.

"Well, you should be."

"How's Katherine?" I asked genuinely.

"She's making it."

"Tell her I said hello."

"I sure will. Well, I gotta get going, but I wanted to speak to you before I left. It was a beautiful wedding. You take care of yourself."

"I will, Aunt Wilma. It was good seeing you again." We hugged each other again and she walked into the crowd. I had only gotten a few more steps when I heard another familiar voice.

"Sara Johnson."

"A-d-a-m!" I screamed when I turned around.

"Hey, baby sis," he said, giving me a hug. "Mama told me about the wedding. I told her I'd try and make it, but not to let you know I was coming."

"Adam, this is the best surprise ever, look at you!" I said, looking him up and down. He looked the exact same, except for a few gray hairs.

"No, look at you. You have done really well for yourself. You look great!"

"This has been one event filled day. Have you seen JaLisa and 'em?"

"Yeah, they are standing over there," he said, pointing. "It looks like they're waiting on you," he said, looking at Shanna. "I'll be around for a couple of days. We got a lot to catch up on."

"We sure do. I'll be right back, don't go anywhere."

"Alright."

When I got to the crowd of girls wanting so badly to catch the bouquet, I noticed all of them whispering. "Are ya'll ready?" Shanna asked.

"We're ready," one of the girls yelled back.

"Ok," she said and turned around. "One, two, three!"

On the count of three, all of the girls ran and I was the only one there to catch the bouquet. "Hey, I'm going to kill ya'll," I said laughing, holding the bouquet. Shanna came over and gave me a hug.

"You know what that means, don't you?"

"Yeah, it means I got to go home and find a vase to put them in," I said, still laughing.

"Mama?" she asked, grabbing my hand.

"Yes, baby?"

"I sure wish Mike was here."

"He is here. See him in my ears, around my neck, and on my arm? And, the place he'll always be, which is in my heart."

"You are an amazing woman, you know that?" she asked, wiping away a tear. "I love you," she said giving me a squeeze.

"I love you, too. Now go. You got a husband over there waiting for you. I'll see you in a bit," I said, shooing her away before I started crying.

"Ok," she said as she walked away.

I looked through the crowd at my mama, who finally made it, my sisters and brothers, Jaylen and Jeremy, and my girlfriends, and realized how blessed I was. As Shanna's limo drove away, I thought back over my life which wasn't an easy journey because there was so much heartache and pain, but through it all, I got the victory. I defeated the odds. I had three beautiful children who I loved very much. Most importantly, I got to experience real love. There was not one day that went by that I didn't think about Mike and I missed him soooo, so much. After his death, there were days I didn't think I was going to make it, but I did. He showed me something that no other man had ever shown me and that was how to be loved, and that love has given me the strength to keep moving forward.

"Girl, did you see that dress she had on?" JaLisa asked, talking about Jacob's girlfriend. "I don't know why they didn't go shopping before they got here, but…" Good ole JaLisa. With her, there was never a dull moment.

Author's Note

I'm sure many of you are wondering why Sara made choices that you and I probably would have never made. She had never been shown love and didn't really know how to love herself and thought she could get that love from Jacob. Although he treated her badly, bad was all she really knew and even though it wasn't acceptable, she thought staying with him was best for her and for her family; after all, where was she going to go?

We may think that staying in an unhealthy relationship is best for our families, but what we're actually doing is hurting them as well as ourselves. We are setting them up to accept that same abuse. Sara was a victim like so many of us. She trusted and believed in a lie. Once there, she felt trapped and had no way out. She did finally find her way though. It took her a while, but she had to wait until she was strong enough and when the time was right, she made her move.

Sara's message to you is no matter how difficult things become, don't give up. You are better than your circumstances. Your situation may be different from hers, but you may be holding yourself back from reaching your fullest potential if you give up because when you do, you automatically lose. There were times when she wanted to give up, but she persevered. She survived verbal and physical abuse, and so can you. Through it all, she pressed forward.

It was unfortunate that the love she had longed for all her life was tragically taken away, but even through the pain of that loss, she was still able to move forward. Ladies, learn how to love yourselves because when you do, it will help when dealing with difficult situations. Men, treat your women like the queens they are. Don't take your loved ones for granted, because we never know what life is going to throw at us and one thing is for sure, we got to keep living.

Lessy'B

LaVergne, TN USA
02 June 2010
184685LV00007B/98/P